"What happened, Skylar?"

She just shook her head, lips trembling, teeth chattering.

"Can you stand?" Cole asked as they neared his door.

"Ye...yes," she said.

He kept an arm around her as he used the key card, then as she sagged, picked her up again and carried her inside. The click of the heavy door behind them came as a relief.

He set her down on the padded bench at the foot of the bed. "Take your clothes off, okay?" he said.

The snow had begun to melt, leaving Skylar wet now, and visibly shaken. Cole stripped off clothes and stopped short. He'd done his best to regard Skylar as a fellow soldier in trouble, done his best to look past the tantalizing curves and creamy flesh to the human being in need beneath the skin.

But seeing her standing there breached all Cole's defenses. Her beauty was fragile, graceful and wonderfully sensual, her body small but lush, breasts modest and perfect, waist tiny and hips curved in a way that jammed his heart in his throat....

And someone had just tried to kill her.

ALICE SHARPE

SOLDIER'S REDEMPTION

This book is dedicated to my sister,

Mary Louise Shumate,

With undying love

Recycling programs
for this product may
not exist in your area.

ISBN-13: 978-0-373-69664-2

SOLDIER'S REDEMPTION

ABOUT THE AUTHOR

Alice Sharpe met her husband-to-be on a cold, foggy beach in Northern California. One year later they were married. Their union has survived the rearing of two children, a handful of earthquakes registering over 6.5, numerous cats and a few special dogs, the latest of which is a yellow Lab named Annie Rose. Alice and her husband now live in a small rural town in Oregon, where she devotes the majority of her time to pursuing her second love, writing.

Alice loves to hear from readers. You can write her c/o Harlequin Books, 233 Broadway, Suite 1001, New York, NY 10279. An SASE for reply is appreciated.

Books by Alice Sharpe

HARLEQUIN INTRIGUE

746—FOR THE SAKE OF THEIR BABY
823—UNDERCOVER BABIES
923—MY SISTER, MYSELF*
929—DUPLICATE DAUGHTER*
1022—ROYAL HEIR
1051—AVENGING ANGEL
1076—THE LAWMAN'S SECRET SON**
1082—BODYGUARD FATHER**
1124—MULTIPLES MYSTERY
1166—AGENT DADDY
1190—A BABY BETWEEN THEM
1209—THE BABY'S BODYGUARD
1304—WESTIN'S WYOMING†
1309—WESTIN LEGACY†
1315—WESTIN FAMILY TIES†
1385—UNDERCOVER MEMORIES‡
1392—MONTANA REFUGE‡
1397—SOLDIER'S REDEMPTION‡

*Dead Ringer
**Skye Brother Babies
†Open Sky Ranch
‡The Legacy

CAST OF CHARACTERS

Cole Bennett—This ex-soldier is in Kanistan for one reason only: to exact retribution on the man responsible for destroying his family. He'll do whatever it takes to accomplish this goal, even if it means breaking his own heart.

Skylar Pope—Fiercely loyal to her family, she's in Kanistan to help her ailing aunt. Meeting a dashing compatriot on one of the worst days of her life is just a happy coincidence, isn't it?

Luca Futura—Skylar's uncle is as ruthless in business dealings as he is kind with his family, especially his wife, to whom he hums a lullaby with a familiar tune. So which is he, gentleman or monster? Or is he both?

Eleanor Ables Futura—A strong artist when healthy, her current treatments have left her fragile and vulnerable. Skylar will protect her, no matter what the cost.

Aneta Cazo—This coworker blames her current distraction on a new romance. It's soon obvious it runs much deeper than that.

Ian Banderas—Futura's assistant is a greedy man with a huge ego. How far will he go to get what he wants?

Svetlana Dacho—A grieving mother desperate to find her missing daughter. She knows exactly who to target. Or does she?

Irina Churo—Cole knows he's lucky this policewoman is almost as determined as he is to get to the truth.

Roman—The man from the past, the man suspected of delivering the fatal blow to Cole's family, the man with the answers, the man no one can find—until now.

Dasha—Who is this striking brunette and what part does she play?

Katerina—A friend of the missing girl, she's decided to get to the bottom of what happened. Now she's scrambling to save her own life.

Chapter One

Skylar Pope opened her aunt's art gallery as she had for most of the past six weeks by unlocking the black wrought-iron gate on the alley-side door and cinching it against the wall. The glass door came next and then the alarm system until at last she was able to enter. The heels of her boots clicked against the polished wood floors as she moved through the workroom into the gallery itself, switching on lights as she strode toward the front of the store.

Once there, she unlocked and opened that door, as well, and stepped out onto the sidewalk of Traterg, carrying with her a sandwich board that advertised the gallery was open for business. She set it up on the sidewalk as usual, shivering as a cold winter wind blew around her legs and teased up the hem of her dress.

Back inside, she returned to the workroom where she took off her coat and deposited that and her shoulder bag in her locker. She took a second to smooth her hair and the dress she'd finished making just the night before, a swirl of lavender and purple with vibrant shots of yellow. The garment was of her own design, one of her better efforts. The fact was she made almost everything she wore with the exception of socks, shoes and underwear. That she hadn't been told to modify her appearance when asked to help out was just another indication of how ill Aunt Eleanor was.

Skylar opened the vault next and took out a tray of jeweled shells that she tucked into a window display along with several glass sculptures. There were a few other pricey items that she retrieved and set in place, delighting in the sparkle and quality of each.

A pot of coffee, very strong, the way most of the citizens of the small Balkan country of Kanistan preferred it, came next. While it brewed, Skylar opened the square pink box she'd brought along from the bakery down the street and arranged jam-filled cookies on a handblown glass platter infused with replications of the small gold-and-red blossoms that were Kanistan's national wildflower. Her aunt had made this piece as she had many of the others in the gallery. A flip of a switch filled the air with Verdi.

The store looked and sounded elegant. It was not exactly to Skylar's taste, which tended to be a little livelier, but it suited her aunt and the mostly kind of stuffy people who came here to purchase art pieces. Skylar thought briefly of getting out her iPod and listening to her own playlist but dismissed the idea. Her job was to greet customers and sell art, not cocoon away behind a sketch pad thinking of new ideas for what she grandly termed her spring collection.

But, hey, she couldn't wait to get going on it. There was lots of downtime after the gallery closed, time when Uncle Luca worked late and her aunt, exhausted from illness and stress, went to bed early. The grays and blacks of the winter city, so different than all the light she was used to in Southern California, continually stirred creative juices that were finding their way into her designs.

For now, she settled down behind the desk to work on

the flyer for the Valentine's Day open house. She was busily moving templates around, wishing Aunt Eleanor was well enough to consult, when the bell over the door alerted her that the first customer of the day had arrived.

She looked up to find two middle-aged women bundled up against the chill. Their coats, hats and gloves looked well-made if dated. By their accents, Skylar judged them to be from closer to the Ukrainian border. Maybe they were on holiday, and maybe they were looking for gifts to take back home.

Skylar had never been a hasty judge of other people, not until she'd taken this job. But in the few short weeks she'd been here, she'd learned to tell a serious collector from a tourist looking for a keepsake, and these two had the look of the latter. Sure enough, they moved quickly past the pricey sculptures and paintings to gather around a central case.

"May I help you?" Skylar asked.

They raised their eyebrows, probably at the accent they could detect in her speech. The taller one asked to see the tray within the case that held an assortment of handblown glass wine stoppers Skylar's aunt had created when she discovered the need for something inexpensive for the casual shopper. Skylar fished the tray out of the case and backed off as the women set about the task of weeding out their favorites.

Skylar glanced at her watch. Aneta was late again, had been all week. She was the local girl Aunt Eleanor employed to help out, but Skylar hadn't found her all that helpful, especially for the past couple of weeks when she'd been distracted and nervous. Aneta had finally confessed she had become involved in a new romance and hinted at trouble. Skylar would have been happy to help if she could, but Aneta's prickly disposition made it tough.

Another jangle of the bell set Skylar's head turning. This time, it was a lone man who entered, pausing inside the door as though scouting out the gallery. As his gaze connected with Skylar's, she felt a small jolt of something akin to recognition although she knew she'd never seen him before.

He didn't look like any other customer she'd ever encountered in this establishment. He was young, not much over thirty, but there was the look of experience in his clear blue eyes that held a challenge, an aura of appraisal, like he was checking out the room in a calculating way and that included her. As though he'd made a decision, he moved toward her with a purpose of step that galvanized her to the spot, his shoulders broad beneath a well-cut dark brown leather jacket that shone with the same richness as his equally dark hair.

The almost imperceptible limp that revealed itself as he walked aroused curiosity and speculation and somehow added to his inherent swagger. She wasn't sure why this guy was here, but she'd wager it had nothing to do with art.

At five foot two, Skylar was already a little on the diminutive side, and when he stopped a few feet away and stared down, his presence was imposing, muscles impressive, expression impossible to read.

"Do you speak English?" he asked.

"Yes," she said, smiling.

"You're American," he said, eyes sparkling as though he'd longed to hear his own language.

"Same as you," she said. She'd known before he opened his mouth that he was a fellow Yank. There was something very U.S. of A. about him, something quietly strong, infinitely self-assured. And maybe something slightly dangerous.

"My name is Cole Bennett. I'm looking for Eleanor Ables," he said, using her aunt's maiden name, the one she'd kept when she'd married three decades before. His voice was deep and sexy and sent a little flutter down her spine. "I'm betting you're not her."

"What gave it away?" Skylar asked with a smile. "The pink stripe in my hair?"

He narrowed his eyes, but there was a glint of humor evident in the slight curve of his lips as his gaze darted up to peruse the stripe. His appraisal traveled down her body to her feet, and he smiled. "I think it might actually be the yellow cowboy boots."

"Maybe I'm an avant-garde kind of artist," she flirted. It was obvious to her that he knew she was playing with him and didn't mind it one bit.

"Maybe you are, but you're also a few decades too young. Are you even out of high school?"

"I beg your pardon," she said. "I'm twenty-five. And a half."

"You look like you're sixteen. And a half."

"I think I'm offended," she said.

His smile ratcheted up a notch. "Didn't mean it that way. Most women are happy to be told they look younger than their years."

"Not when it plunges them into jailbait territory," she said. "Anyway, as you so astutely discerned, I am not Eleanor Ables. I'm filling in for her. May I help you?"

"How about a name?"

"Skylar Pope." Skylar suddenly became aware that the other customers had moved to the counter with their choices and had discreetly approached the cookie plate. "Excuse me a minute," she said and hurried over to help them, aware that Cole Bennett's gaze tracked every move she made.

Skylar chatted warmly with the customers as she wrapped each modest purchase as though it was a Picasso, per her aunt's long-standing tradition. After the women left, she looked around to see where Cole had wandered off to and found him studying a shelf of glass displayed against a roughly hewn wooden wall. She decided to give him space. It took him a few minutes, but eventually he sought her out again. She offered him coffee and a cookie.

"Thanks," he said, accepting the coffee, watching her as she dropped a single sugar cube in it as requested. "You speak the language very well."

"Years of practice," she said. "Unless I get careless, most people can't tell I'm from somewhere else."

"And where is that somewhere else?"

"California, but I spent a week or two here each summer when I was growing up." She tilted her head and added, "Do you know my aunt, Mr. Bennett?"

"Eleanor Ables is your aunt?"

"Yes, my father's sister."

He took a sip, and she struggled to ignore the way his muscles moved under the soft leather of his jacket, the snug fit of the soft black shirt against his trim torso. Hopeless not to notice those things, however. She'd never designed men's clothes, but she bet he'd look fabulous in anything he wore.

"Call me Cole," he said. "And, no, I've never had the pleasure. A friend of mine visited Traterg last year and brought home the most unique glass figurine. He raved about the woman who had created and sold it to him. When I found myself in Kanistan, I decided to come meet the artist and see if I could find something equally tempting for myself."

She looked up into his eyes. Everything he'd just said sounded as though he'd rehearsed it. She almost called him on it but stopped herself short. He was a customer, and he'd been looking at very expensive pieces. What did she care if he made up a story about why he wanted one?

"Has anything in particular caught your eye?" she asked and felt warmth in her face as his gaze lingered on her mouth. *Now who was flirting?*

"Tell me about this display," he said, setting the cup aside and leading the way back to the wooden wall.

For the next forty-five minutes, Skylar showed Cole just about everything in the gallery, starting with her aunt's tree of life theme, the pieces of which ran the gamut from an intricate vase to a huge handblown tree with a thousand individual leaves to a dozen other more modest pieces. As they moved from that to artwork to jewelry, she answered a dozen questions about the artists, their procedures and about herself. His curiosity in everything seemed genuine and as sincere as the unacknowledged dance going on between them as they spoke. They were in the middle of considering colorful three-dimensional glass elliptical shapes that were reminiscent of the famous Fabergé eggs when the bell at the door announced a new customer.

This time, Skylar recognized the man as an elderly collector who had come in ten days before to choose a different frame for his miniature painting. They'd spent a satisfying couple of hours judging the merits of this one over that. Skylar wasn't an artist per se, but she did understand color and proportions.

"Mr. Machnik, how nice to see you," she said in English as she knew he appreciated practicing his when he could. "I bet you're here to pick up your Bartow."

"Yes, yes, I've missed it hanging in my parlor," he said, his speech heavily accented. Bushy white eyebrows lifted over light gray eyes as he added, "It is back yet?"

"Yes, it came back yesterday, and I have to admit I took a peek. You were right to insist on the gilt. The gold in the frame perfectly reflects the light in the sky. It's waiting for you in the vault. I'll be right back." She excused herself to go get it, anxious to conclude this transaction before Cole Bennett got bored and left without buying something.

The painting was where she'd left it, wrapped in brown paper, about twelve square inches including the frame. She took it from the shelf and returned to the showroom, meeting Mr. Machnik at the counter where she carefully peeled away the invoice and the brown paper surrounding his treasure.

Machnik and she both gasped in the same instant. "Is this a joke?" he choked out.

Skylar looked at the ornate gilt frame she'd rewrapped when it returned from the workshop the afternoon before and felt her pulse quicken. The beautiful rendition of a bucolic hilltop was gone, replaced with a blank rectangle of cardboard.

"I don't understand," she said.

"Where is my painting?" he demanded as the kindly veneer flaked away from his voice.

"I don't know," she said, looking around the gallery as though it might have walked out of the vault on its own and hidden behind a sculpture. "It was in this frame yesterday." She met Cole's gaze and flinched at the intensity of his stare as he obviously eavesdropped.

"I demand to know what's going on," Machnik said. "I paid fifty thousand euros for that painting, and as you know, it is worth double that now, maybe triple."

Her attention flicked back to Machnik. "I know, sir. All I can think is that Aneta may have mistakenly rotated it back into the gallery." It was possible although Aneta was seldom alone here for long. Still, there was no doubting Aneta was acting flaky as of late. "I assure you, I'll look into this right away. Let me get you a cup of coffee."

"No, thank you," he said, checking his pocket watch. "I'm going to be late for an appointment. I will be back at four o'clock, and I expect to find my painting waiting for me."

"Yes, I understand," Skylar said, her voice shaking. She was already punching Aneta's number into her phone.

Aneta answered on the first ring as though she'd been waiting for a call. "Thank goodness you're there," Skylar said as the bell jangled, signaling Machnik exiting the shop. She was vaguely aware of Cole following the older man to the door and cursed the events of the past few minutes.

"I cannot speak," Aneta said.

"You have to," Skylar insisted. "What do you know about Oleskii Machnik's painting, the one in the vault?"

"What! I know nothing," Aneta insisted. "I'm hanging up."

"No, wait. It's missing, Aneta. The Bartow miniature was in the safe when I left yesterday, and now it's gone. Just the frame remains. Did you move it?"

"I cannot speak," Aneta repeated, her voice dropping.

"What do you mean? Why aren't you here at the gallery? What's going on?" Skylar stopped asking questions as she realized Aneta had disconnected.

Skylar hit Redial, but there was no answer this time. She wanted to throw the phone in frustration. If she didn't find a rational reason for this situation, her aunt would have to be told and that would bring in the police.

She raced back to the vault, shoving things aside, opening other packages. Had she made a mistake? Had she inadvertently misplaced it herself?

"Can I help?" Cole Bennett asked from the doorway.

She looked up at him, shock robbing her of her voice. She'd forgotten about him. She wasn't sure what to do now, who to contact.

"I couldn't help overhearing just about everything," Cole continued as though recognizing her inability to form a coherent sentence.

She stared at him, still speechless.

"I've taken the liberty of locking your front door and turning the open sign to closed. It seems your coworker knows something."

That jarred words back into her mouth. "How could you possibly know what she said?"

"I just gathered as much from your end of the conversation. Am I right?"

"I think so, but she won't talk to me. We have trouble with each other on the phone."

"Then you have to see her face-to-face. Do you know where she lives?"

"I know the address. I mean, I can find it. It's in the book over on the desk. But I'll have to call a cab or find the right bus."

"Or call a friend."

"I don't have many friends here, just family," she said, hurrying to the desk and finding Aneta's address. She had no idea what part of the city it was in, but she copied it quickly.

"Your aunt—"

"She mustn't hear a word of this."

"I got the feeling Mr. Machnik will not meekly accept the loss of something he cares about," he added. "And what did he mean it's worth double or triple what he paid?"

"The artist died earlier this year. The prices on his miniatures skyrocketed. I'll have to find the painting or make retribution somehow." She gulped her panic and wondered about insurance, but more than that, she wondered how the painting could have disappeared from a locked vault....

"Your aunt—"

"I can't tell my aunt. She's undergoing chemotherapy. She's too sick to be involved."

"I'm sorry," he said, his voice compassionate and yet in control. "Well, here's an idea. I have a rental outside. I'll give you a ride."

"I can't ask—"

"I don't believe you did. Are you coming?"

It took Skylar one heartbeat to review her options. She locked the vault and the store. A minute later, she slid into his rental, her heart jammed high in her throat.

Chapter Two

It turned out Skylar's coworker lived thirty minutes away in a cinder block apartment building with a rusty black fire escape zigzagging its way from the top floor to the bottom. The small, unlocked lobby was dark and held only a row of mailboxes. Cole and Skylar stood side by side looking at the names, searching for Aneta's apartment number and floor.

Cole's original plan upon entering the art gallery had been to flirt his way into a dinner invitation with Luca Futura's niece. He'd been well on his way to accomplishing that goal when the missing painting provided a solid plan B. Cole was used to taking opportunities as they presented themselves. He was former special forces, and that meant augmenting years of physical and mental training with split-second tactical decision making.

Now, hopefully, Skylar would see him as a friend, a confidant, someone who'd been willing to lend her a hand…someone she could trust.

He'd chosen Skylar for his mission because she appeared to be the weakest link in Futura's chain—and as such, Cole's best chance of getting close to a man shielded behind layers of protection.

He'd done his research, and he knew Skylar was a recent graduate of a design school. She had three brothers and a sister plus a large extended family spread all over the States. She created clothes for a living and wore them like a petite fashion model, tended to change her hair color on a whim and worked whatever odd jobs paid the bills and gave her time to do what she loved.

He'd known all that going in. What he hadn't known was how damn pretty she was up close and personal, the way her eyes resembled blue diamonds, the creamy texture of her almost translucent pale skin, the fullness of her lips or the rounded curves of breasts and hips that merged into a trim waist.

Totally feminine and utterly breathtaking—and this from a man who didn't often allow a person's appearance to affect him.

But it wasn't just her looks…there was something else, something robust and lively about her. She'd flirted with him with ease, yet she had no hidden agenda like he did. She just seemed to like people. And there was the way she'd faced first the disappearance of the painting and then her customer's threats with polite courage, and that had touched him. And to be honest, her distress alarmed him.

He'd been prepared to use her in whatever way presented itself; he wasn't prepared to actually feel something for her.

"Here it is. Aneta Cazo, fifth floor," Skylar said, tapping one of the boxes. "Apartment 509."

He followed her up the gloomy stairs, enjoying the way her dress hugged her rear, then flared to fall softly against her legs, the natural sway of her hips as she moved. She wore some fragrance that wafted back at him as she climbed, sort of summery and flowery but not too strong. She belonged in a place of light and outshone these somber surroundings like a sun drop in a cave. He dragged his mind back to his job. They would convince Aneta to go back to the gallery with them and produce the painting, which she must have taken out of the frame for some crazy reason, then he would ask Skylar out to dinner, maybe at his hotel, maybe chance a kiss good-night so she would understand he was interested in seeing more of her.

The door was closed, and Skylar rapped against the wood. No one responded, so she called out Aneta's name and they waited.

Cole heard a sound coming from inside, a sound he couldn't identify, but it raised instincts honed over many years. He reached around Skylar and tried the knob. It turned in his hand. Soundlessly, he put an arm back to keep Skylar behind him and opened the door.

In one glimpse, he took in two things about the drab apartment. One was a young woman with short brown hair lying on the floor, her white blouse stained red over her heart. The second was a sound coming from behind a closed door to his right. Skylar immediately dashed past him to the woman and fell to her knees. Words of caution died on Cole's lips as he crossed to the connecting door and opened it. The bedroom beyond was tidy and predictable except for an open suitcase on the bed and a curtain blowing into the room at the window.

He ran to look outside and found someone running down the fire escape. The guy had a pretty good head start, but Cole climbed out and took off after him, hoping the structure was a lot sturdier than it had appeared from a distance or felt now that he was on it.

The man looked over his shoulder to track Cole, but he was too far away for Cole to make out his features. He wore a dark, hooded jacket that obscured even his coloring. Cole took the steps two at a time, adrenaline helping to mask the pain in his leg. While Cole was still two stories up, the man jumped the final few feet to the sidewalk and ran to a black car that sped away as Cole came to a grinding halt still one floor above the ground.

He watched the car turn right at the first corner, then re-climbed the stairs as quickly as he could, hoping that leaving Skylar alone hadn't been a mistake. Once through the window, he paused by the suitcase where he found a few items that looked as though they'd been thrown in without care and a few others lying beside the suitcase as though awaiting their turn.

Skylar was still kneeling on the floor beside the woman although now she sat with her hands resting against her own legs, tears rolling down her cheeks.

She looked up at him, lips trembling.

He didn't need to ask, but he did anyway. "Is she—"

"Yes. She's dead."

Skylar was treated with cool detachment by the police, which included a detective named Kilo who spoke excellent English. Still there were questions to be answered— lots of them. She did her best to explain things as well as she could, but there was so much she was confused about.

Did Aneta's murder have anything to do with the mysterious disappearance of Mr. Machnik's painting? How could two such startling events not be connected?

Through it all, Cole stuck by her side, his presence as rock solid as his muscles. The police asked him a few questions about himself and his reasons for being in Kanistan, and from his answers, she gleaned he was here on business, that his business had something to with imports and exports and perhaps that explained his original interest in the gallery.

When it came to personal details, he seemed to be open and yet vague. Skylar didn't know him well enough to say whether he was actually being obtuse or just private, a man caught up in someone else's drama maybe or beginning to seriously regret an impulsive offer to help out.

He explained about the chase, as well, describing the man as under six feet wearing dark clothes, age unknown but not too old—going by the way he moved and jumped.

"And he escaped in a car with Kanistan plates?" Kilo quizzed.

"Yes."

"What color?"

"Black. It looked like a late-model Mercedes to me but I'm not sure."

The detective turned his attention back to Skylar. "You say she had a new lover?" A nearby officer stood poised, pen in hand, to take notes. Kilo himself was on the small side with freckled skin and thinning hair, a wispy mustache accenting a long face. By the outline of a package of cigarettes showing beneath the fabric of his brown suit pocket and the way his hand kept returning to pat it, she assumed he was dying for a smoke. She guessed there must be some rule about fouling a murder scene with smoke and ashes.

"Yes."

"For how long?"

"Not long. A couple of weeks maybe."

"His name?"

"She never said his name."

"What did he look like?"

"I never saw him," she said.

The detective patted the cigarette package as he narrowed his eyes. "He never came to pick her up for a date or a coffee?"

"No."

"Think for a moment," he coaxed as his hand dropped

from his pocket. "Did you get the feeling she was hiding his identity, as though, perhaps, he was a married man?"

Skylar thought. The truth was that she and Aneta had not been close, had shared few if any confidences and that Skylar didn't really know her. Had she been friendlier the first couple of weeks Skylar was here? Marginally, maybe. "I can't be sure," she said, "but I guess it's possible."

The detective and the uniformed officer exchanged glances. Kilo shrugged. "Her suitcase is half packed as though she was leaving. A jealous lover, a rendezvous, dissension between thieves? Who knows? We will need to meet you back at your shop and look for the missing painting," the detective continued. "My men will search this apartment when forensics is finished to make sure Ms. Cazo did not steal it and bring it here. That is, if her killer did not take it with him when he fled."

Skylar started to protest but didn't. How did she know what Aneta would or wouldn't do?"

"And you should contact the owner of your gallery at once."

"No! The owner is my aunt, Eleanor Ables, and she's not well. She can't hear news like this on the phone."

"Eleanor Ables? You are talking about Luca Futura's wife?"

"Yes."

"Luca Futura is your uncle?"

"Yes."

"And why did you not mention this at once?"

"I don't want to bother my uncle."

The detective waved away her concern. "He must be told." He turned to the uniformed officer and snapped off a few words. The twitch in Kilo's jaw signaled the regard in which Skylar's uncle was held. "We will contact him at once," he said, turning back to Skylar.

"If you must," Skylar said.

"You may go now. We can give you a lift back to the gallery."

"That's okay. I'll take her," Cole said from her side.

The thought of thirty minutes in the car with Kilo as he played catch-up to his nicotine deprivation was enough to sway Skylar's decision in Cole's favor though she was pretty sure she shouldn't be leaning so heavily on a stranger. But Cole didn't seem like much of a stranger anymore. Since arriving in Traterg, she'd spent her days at the shop and her evenings with her aunt and uncle when he was home. There'd been no opportunity to make friends—only Aneta who hadn't been the warmest woman in the world.

Skylar flinched as guilt prickled her skin. Aneta was about the same age as Skylar and her life was over, destroyed by someone who had made sure she'd never see another birthday.

Cole touched her arm and she jumped. "Ready to go?" he asked, and she turned to see that people had arrived to take away Aneta's body.

Cole's limp seemed more pronounced as they walked down the stairs. Once in his car, Skylar lay back against the headrest and closed her eyes, relieved to be away from the murder scene, the police and the strain of the past hour.

"Are you okay?" Cole asked.

She opened her eyes and found him looking at her. He was an imposing-looking man in his way, yet his eyes showed kindness. She wished she knew him better, wished she could seek comfort in his arms, draw heat from his body. In other words, a hug would be nice....

"I really don't want to go back to the gallery," she said.

"Where do you want to go, then?"

"Anywhere else," she said and then smiled. "I'm just

dreaming. I have to meet the police, and my uncle will want details. I have to go back. I just don't want to."

"Just who is your uncle?" Cole said as he pulled away from the curb. "That detective sure seemed to snap to order when you mentioned his name."

"Uncle Luca is high up in Traterg government," she said. "Like a mayor or something. I don't understand the politics here, but I know he's held in high esteem."

"Then he'll be able to help deal with the man whose painting went missing."

"I'm sure he can. I wonder what Aneta did with it."

"Is there any chance someone else might have taken it?"

"There is no one else. It's just me and Aneta. I opened the store this morning—there was no sign of a break-in. And Aneta is never there alone, and I have the only key. She must have slipped the painting out of the frame and vault while I was in the bathroom and hidden it away to carry out when she left."

"Your setup sounds kind of unusual."

"My aunt is very cautious. She's always taken care of the gallery herself until now, and she made it clear I was to conduct all business transactions myself. Man, what a mess."

"It's not your fault," he said as he guided the car through early afternoon traffic.

"I feel responsible, though," she said.

"The plight of the conscientious," he murmured.

She stared at his profile a moment. "Why are you going out of your way to help me?" she said at last.

He cast her a quick glance. "Take a look in the mirror sometime."

"What does that mean?"

"It means you are an exceptionally pretty woman."

"So you're helping me because you think I'm pretty?"

"You sound disappointed."

"I hoped maybe it was my keen sense of fashion."

That got a smile out of him. "That, too. No, really, you needed help and then things went nuts and you needed more help and I was glad to be able to offer it."

"What happened to your leg?"

He was quiet so long she was on the verge of apologizing for prying. "Bullets," he finally said.

"Ouch. Were you with the police, or were you on the other side?"

He smiled again. "Soldier, and if you don't mind, I'd rather not talk about it."

"But that explains why you chased after a killer."

"I guess."

"Because I don't think that's the normal response for everyone. He must have had a gun. He might have turned around and shot you."

"That's true. I guess you owe me something for all my helpful bravery."

She smiled this time. "You didn't actually catch him."

"Details. I suggest you keep me company tonight over dinner."

"And that will wipe the slate clean?"

This time he looked at her with smoldering eyes, and she felt a jab of heat in her groin. It had been a long time since she'd been in a serious relationship.

"I'm a businessman alone in a strange city with an evening to kill," he said. Then he swore under his breath. "Sorry, poor choice of words."

"It's okay," she said, but the mention of killing did somber her mood once again. Thankfully they were just pulling up in the alley behind the gallery. "Thanks for all your help," she said, her hand already on the door handle.

But he got out, too. "I'm coming with you," he said over the top of the car.

"I don't think—"

"Do you really, really want to go into that shop alone and wait for the police by yourself?" he asked, that intense look back in his blue eyes as he rounded the trunk to stop a foot in front of her.

She looked up at him, her throat suddenly swollen. There was something going on with him that she couldn't pin down. On the other hand, she really, really didn't want to be alone in the gallery.

He surprised her then by gripping her arms and pulling her close to him until her head came to a rest right under his chin. Slowly, almost tenderly, his arms wrapped around her, his body heat enveloping her. She had the sudden and very strong feeling he was going to kiss her, and she gazed up at him. His lips looked soft and inviting, and her own tingled with anticipation. When he did nothing, she looked beyond his mouth and found his expression pensive.

"What's the hug for?" she whispered.

"You just looked like you needed one."

As she unlocked the door, his arm slipped around her shoulders. She did nothing to dislodge it.

Chapter Three

Cole tried to stay out of the way while Skylar and the cops searched for some sign of the missing painting. He planted himself by the vase he'd looked at earlier, such a fragile and fanciful shape it was hard to believe it had started from a combination of fire and sand.

He had a lot to think about to keep him busy. If what he suspected about Luca Futura's role in this city was true, it seemed unlikely he wasn't involved with the murder, but in what way? Why would he steal something out of his own wife's store? Sure, the little painting was apparently quite valuable but not worth a fortune—not to someone like Futura. Had he asked Aneta to take it and then killed her? Again, why?

Or had Aneta been working on her own? Had Futura found out somehow that Aneta was a thief? Did he kill her out of vengeance or send someone to do his dirty work instead of involving the police?

But why do all that when he all but owned the Traterg police? The former chief, a man by the name of Alexie Smirnoff, might be dead, but Cole knew Futura had replaced him almost immediately, promoting from within a network of government workers to find the next man whom he could no doubt manipulate into doing what he wanted. So why resort to murder that would require an investigation?

It was obvious to Cole that Skylar Pope didn't have the slightest idea just how powerful and corrupt her uncle Luca truly was. She was in for some major eye-opening in the near future. And he knew it would be terrible for her, not perhaps because of her deep love for her uncle but on her aunt's behalf.

So the question became the true nature of Detective Kilo. Was he an honest man, a crook or worse?

"Is anything else missing?" the detective asked Skylar, and Cole leaned forward, anxious to hear her response.

"I can't tell without doing a complete inventory, which I'll start tomorrow," Skylar said. "But offhand, nothing seems out of place except that painting. Oh my gosh, I am going to have to call Mr. Machnik. He's going to come unglued."

"We can do that for you," the detective said.

"No, I'll do it, thanks," Skylar said. "He deserves to hear the news from me."

"We examined Ms. Cazo's apartment and found nothing of interest," Detective Kilo continued. He took out a package of cigarettes.

"No smoking in the gallery," Skylar said. "How…how did Aneta die? Was it a gun? Was it quick?"

"I can't discuss that right now," Kilo said, repocketing the packet. "You understand."

"I suppose," she said, and Cole noticed she rubbed her hands on her dress as though washing away invisible blood.

A few minutes later, a knock on the locked front door heralded a new arrival. One of the policemen opened it. By the deferential look on the officer's face as he turned back into the room, Cole suspected he was about to come face-to-face with Skylar's uncle.

Would Futura recognize Cole? Would he see something of Cole's father in his face, and would his razor-sharp brain leap to make connections Cole hadn't anticipated?

As for what Futura looked like…Cole had seen pictures, both a candid shot his brother had taken with his cell phone months before and a few from articles written about him on the internet. Nowadays, the man stayed out of the spotlight, but he was still an imposing and singular-looking guy, and as he entered the shop, his presence dominated the room.

Suave and handsome, even in his late sixties, Luca's head seemed a little too large for his body. Cole had read that many actors and performers shared this trait of a large head and, hence, a larger face where emotions and reactions could be discerned by cameras and audiences from a distance.

Futura's body looked strong, as well—back straight, hands large, fingers tapered. Cole's gaze went at once to his right hand ring finger where he found what he'd been told to expect: a gold band inlaid with onyx in the shape of an owl.

He raised his gaze and found Futura returning the appraisal. The man's instincts had immediately zeroed in on the one person in the gallery who didn't seem to fit. A chill ran down Cole's spine.

Futura's icy-gray eyes were about the same color as the impeccably made suit that draped his flesh. His tie was white, his overcoat black and in his hands he held a black bowler, a style of hat not seen much anymore.

"Uncle Luca, thank goodness you're here," Skylar said and hurried to Futura who wrapped her in a hug. This warmth between them shocked Cole, who had expected his own distaste of the man, hatred even, would be a universal reaction. But Skylar obviously didn't share these feelings.

Nor did the police who all seemed to snap to attention, vying with one another to bring Futura up to speed both in English and in the language of Kanistan. Once the known details were apparently related, Futura told Skylar to get her things and that he would see she returned home at once.

And then he turned his attention back to Cole although Cole would have bet it had never strayed too far away. "And just who are you, again?" he asked.

Cole introduced himself, stepping forward and offering a hand. Luca shook it, his grip strong and unyielding. His light eyes betrayed nothing of what he thought.

"Cole has been wonderful during this whole ordeal," Skylar said, casting Cole a warm smile. "I would have been lost without his help."

"Then we must repay him," Luca said, replacing his hat and reaching inside his chest pocket to take out a large, flat wallet. He fished a wad of cash out and offered it to Cole, who shook his head gently.

"I wouldn't dream of taking money for what little I did. I was happy to help," he said.

"Then you must come to dinner," Futura said.

Cole smiled. "It's not necessary."

"I insist," Futura said as he replaced the money in his wallet. "How long will you be in Traterg, Mr. Bennett?"

"A week, perhaps," Cole said.

"Tomorrow night, then? Around seven?"

"I wouldn't want to be an imposition."

"I told him about Aunt Eleanor," Skylar interjected, with a wary glance at her uncle.

"Ah. Well, then, Mr. Bennett, perhaps you will understand it better when I say that my wife would appreciate meeting a man of such chivalry, especially in regard to her favorite niece and her beloved gallery. I would invite you tonight, but I believe Skylar and I must hurry home now and tell Eleanor of the sad news concerning Ms. Cazo."

"And the missing painting," Skylar said, eyes downcast.

"The police will find who took the painting, and if it cannot be recovered, the gallery's insurance policy will cover the theft. Please, do as I ask, and get your things while I have a final word with the detective."

"I'll go with you," Cole said, glancing at Skylar first, then the police. "My car is parked out back in the alley. Is it okay if I leave now?"

"We know how to reach you should the need arise," Detective Kilo said.

Cole followed Skylar into the back room where she once again retrieved her personal belongings from her locker. She walked him to the back door, twisting the lock, then looking up into his eyes before opening it. "You don't have to come to dinner," she said. "Uncle Luca is used to getting what he wants, but he'll understand."

"I want to. Your uncle is very persuasive."

"Yes, he is."

"But I wish you could meet at the hotel tonight for a late supper. Can you do that, Skylar?"

She hesitated a moment as though thinking. "I don't think I can," she finally said.

He lowered his voice, leaning closer so she could hear him. "I'm staying at the Hotel Traterg, room 1311. I'll make a reservation at the restaurant downstairs for, say, nine o'clock." He brushed her forehead with his lips and added, "Come if you can, okay?"

"My uncle isn't the only persuasive one," she murmured, looking down at his hand, which had landed on her arm as he spoke. She glanced back up into his eyes, and he felt a stirring in his gut and the crazy desire to touch his lips with hers. She was just so damn lovely and so vulnerable—much more so than she even knew.

"I don't know a thing about you," she added.

"Not true," he countered, his voice as soft as hers. "You know I chase after killers and can drive on the right *and* the left side of the road." He allowed his gaze to devour her as he added, "And you know that I have an appreciation for…beauty…in all its infinite forms. Say you'll try to come."

"I'll try," she whispered.

He left before he could change his mind and tell her to run like the wind.

ELEANOR ABLES HAD ALWAYS BEEN larger than life to Skylar—not only tall but elegant and artistic in everything she did from decorating her home to cooking a meal to blowing glass and running a gallery.

Now, in the middle of treatments, she was still a beauty, but it was of a frailer, more fragile nature, reminding Skylar more of her grandmother than ever before.

Aunt Eleanor took the news of Aneta's death with stoic grace, but the troubled look in her dark blue eyes was a clear indication of how disturbed she was. She kept repeating Aneta couldn't have stolen the painting, yet what other possibilities were there? The store had not been broken into, and there was that half-packed suitcase at Aneta's apartment as though she'd been caught in the act of leaving Traterg.

Skylar sat with her aunt for two hours, consoling her, reading to her until at last the older woman closed her eyes and fell into a deep sleep enhanced with a sleeping aid. She would be out for the rest of the night.

Uncle Luca had left after receiving a call. Skylar startled when he opened the door and spoke from the hall. The house was so big that there were never any of the ordinary sounds like a garage door opener or doors closing or even footsteps in the hall to forewarn her when someone approached. "She's asleep?" he asked.

Skylar laid the book aside, turned down the lamp and nodded at the nurse who sat knitting by the window. She joined her uncle and closed the door behind her. "Yes."

"How did she take the news of Aneta's death?"

"Not well."

"I should have told Ian I couldn't come tonight. I should have stayed with Eleanor."

Skylar patted his arm. "Don't torture yourself, Uncle Luca." She spoke his language as she always did when she was staying in his house unless there were people present who didn't understand it. "Aunt Eleanor needs sleep now, and you'll be here in the morning. Shall I have the cook reheat your dinner, or would you just like a sandwich sent up to your study?"

"The sandwich will be fine, then I'll turn in early and catch up on paperwork. By the way, I've started a background check on Cole Bennett."

Skylar glanced up at him, startled. "A background check? Why?"

"You don't think I would allow someone into my home without knowing who and what he really is, do you?"

"I guess not."

"And really, is it just a coincidence he was at the gallery ready to offer a helping hand at the very moment you needed one?"

"Yes, I think it is," she said. "He'd been there for an hour or more."

Her uncle took off his suit jacket and draped it over one arm. "Still, I am a prudent man. One does not manage to stay afloat in this government if they are not cautious. Now, are you going to your room to sketch?"

"I may. But first I'll go talk to the cook."

He leaned down and kissed her cheek. "Thank you, Skylar. You're a great comfort to both your aunt and myself right now."

She smiled in response and watched as he walked off down the hall. Then she hurried toward the kitchen where she passed along her uncle's wishes to the cook.

Upstairs in her own room, which was about as large as her whole place back home, she took out her sketch pad and lay across the bed, pencil poised over paper, mind a million miles away.

She kept seeing Aneta's still face in her dark little apartment. The girl had always shown up at work looking put together in surprisingly well-made clothes. Her modest apartment had come as quite a shock to Skylar, who had assumed from the way Aneta dressed that she was better off than that. After a few minutes of thought, Skylar came up with an explanation: she was almost positive some of Aneta's clothes—like the silver knit dress she'd worn the day before—had once belonged to Aunt Eleanor. Did Aunt Eleanor know something about Aneta that would help the police find her killer? Would anyone think to ask her?

And then there was that whole weird phone conversation. Had Aneta been flippant or frightened? Could Skylar have helped her if she'd worked harder at becoming her friend?

Her gaze darted to the clock. It was only eight o'clock,

and Cole had said he'd make a reservation for nine. Skylar turned over on her back, sketch pad forgotten. By tomorrow, her uncle would have done a thorough background check on Cole, and perhaps he would have decided Cole wasn't "safe" enough to have at the house. She might never see him again.

Never look into those blue eyes or find out if his lips lived up to their promise or feel his heat as he held her. The thought of missing all that made her stomach twist.

And face it—there was more to him than met the eye, and she was dying to know what it meant.

NINE O'CLOCK CAME and went. She wasn't coming. He'd have to wait until tomorrow night to see her, or she might get the feeling he was pushing her and she'd back off.

In a way, Cole was glad to have a reprieve from this charade. He caught a glimpse of something bright and cheerful staring at him from atop the dresser, and he crossed the room to pick it up and look at it.

The figurine was that of a clown, half child's toy, half trinket. About six inches high and made of some kind of resin draped with cloth, the clown wore a one-piece suit, half red, half yellow, both dotted with green. He had big shoes, a red nose, orange hair and a purple balloon suspended on a wire "string." The wire was the weak point and had broken many times over the years, but Cole had always glued it back in place, marveling that anyone would have bought something like this for little more than a baby. Amazing he hadn't poked his eye out on the thing.

He'd had it forever.

Now he tucked it in the top drawer and closed it away from view right as a knock sounded on the hall door. Probably the maid to turn down the bed. His stomach grumbled, so he grabbed his leather jacket and pulled it

on, intending to find a bite down in the restaurant while
the maid did her thing. But it wasn't the maid at the door.

His quickening pulse as he looked down and found
Skylar looking up at him should have sent cascading
alarms all through his head. He smiled instead. "You
came."

"I'm sorry I'm late. I had to stop by the gallery."

She looked wonderful in her bright red coat with a
black velvet collar, her cheeks pink from the cold outside, her hair blond and shiny. He took her shoulders in
his hands and pulled her into his arms, surprising both of
them with the gesture. Without giving it another moment's
thought, he bent down and kissed her, and if she was
amazed at his audacity, she didn't show it. Instead, she
returned his kiss, her body pressed close to his, her arm
around his shoulder, her fingertips touching the back of
his neck, her lips parting, her tongue smooth against his.

Had he ever wanted a woman this quickly and completely? Never, he knew that. The alarm that should have
gone off with his first glimpse of her finally rang clear
in his head, and he ended the kiss before it was too late
for both of them.

"Do you always move this fast?" she asked, her cheeks
even rosier as she touched his chest with one hand and
the other lit against her own, a curiously intimate gesture
that got to him for a moment.

He swallowed hard, working now to get back the control he shouldn't have lost in the first place. "Never," he
said, and that was the most truthful word he'd ever uttered.
But this wasn't love and romance. This was a skirmish in
a battle, and control had to be taken quickly and firmly.

"I see. I guess. Am I too late?" she asked.

"Too late for what?"

"Dinner, silly."

He smiled into her eyes. "No."

"Good, because I'm really hungry."

"So am I," he said, closing the door behind him. He took her hand in his and led her toward the elevator. "So am I."

Chapter Four

"What's this for?" Cole asked as Skylar handed him a box she took from her handbag. She'd stopped by the gallery before coming to the hotel and presented her gift right after the waiter had taken their drink order.

"Open it," she coaxed. He met her gaze and then began peeling away the thick sage-green paper to reveal a tan box. The lid came next, and then a smile lit his face as he stared down into the box and back at her.

"Skylar, you shouldn't have—"

"Thanked you for helping me?" she interrupted. "Oh, yes, I should."

He plucked the heavy paperweight out of the box and cradled it in his hand. Within the globe of glass resided a tree, its delicate branches dotted with white flowers and dark green leaves, a hint of blue for the sky and shades of rust for its roots. It was one her aunt's most exquisite pieces, and Skylar warmed at the sight of Cole's obvious pleasure.

"This is beautiful," he said. "Thank you."

"It's one of her smaller pieces, but I didn't want to give you something so big it would be a problem getting it back to the States. By the way, where do you live?"

"Nevada," he said. "Las Vegas." He stared at her a second and added, "You look surprised."

"I guess I just never thought an import/export business would be based in Las Vegas."

"In today's world, it doesn't matter much where you're based."

The waiter appeared with wine for her, a draft beer for him. As he disappeared into the polished woodwork, Cole and Skylar clinked glasses. "Here's to chance meetings," he said. "Although I thought for sure they'd card you when you ordered wine."

"I do get carded in the States a lot, but Europe is different."

He smiled again, and with that slight movement of his lips, the full memory of his earlier kiss swamped her. She quickly opened her menu, alarmed by her own lustful thoughts, her mind more on his bed upstairs than on the list of entrées before her.

Maybe it was the awfulness of the day that had set her mind wandering like this. Or maybe it was his obvious attraction to her that seemed unexpected and yet genuine…and very reciprocated on her part.

"What sounds good?" he asked, and she looked up to see him folding the menu and laying it aside.

"I'm not sure," she said. "How about you?"

"I've heard the chef is a master with pasta. I think I'll try the clam linguine."

She folded her menu, as well. "I'll have the same."

They gave their dinner order and then were alone again—or as alone as two people in a bustling restaurant can be. Still, it was an old-fashioned place, a little staunch and very respectable, and the tables were a discreet distance from each other. The empty table closest to theirs sported a reserved place card that Skylar hoped would remain as long as they were there.

For a while, they talked about themselves in general,

getting-to-know-you terms, comparing colleges and families, tastes in books and movies, ordinary things. She found out his mother was dead and his father and he were estranged. Skylar couldn't imagine such a thing. No siblings, no parents—how could he stand being so alone? She also discovered he'd served in the military, but he didn't mention his injury and she didn't ask. He'd been out just a few months, he said, and there was a wistful sound to his voice that alerted her to the fact he hadn't left because he wanted to but because he'd had no choice and that it hurt him.

Their dinners arrived quicker than she'd anticipated. She stole candlelit looks at his face as he tasted the wine the waiter poured for him to approve, wondering how someone so young could come across so mature. Lots of the men she knew were a few years older than him, and they all seemed to be stuck in some Peter Pan perpetual youth thing while this guy was a grown-up through and through—the kind of man a woman could depend on. He'd proven that today.

Whoa. Her thoughts were way ahead of her. Maybe the wine had gone straight to her head.

She and Cole were expounding the virtues of the linguine when the party for the table behind Cole was seated. It consisted of a man and a woman, and to Skylar's surprise, she recognized the male as her uncle's pompous secretary and right-hand man. She ducked her head as he sat down, his back to her.

Cole leaned forward. "What's wrong? Do you know those people?"

"Just one of them," she replied, her voice little more than a whisper.

"Which one?"

"The man. He's sitting right behind you."

"The guy with the slicked back blond hair and glasses? The one with the mole on his left cheek?" His voice was as soft as hers.

"Yes," she said, amazed that Cole had noticed so many details when he couldn't have had more than a glimpse of him in passing.

"Who is he?"

"He works for my uncle. His name is Ian Banderas."

"Who's the woman?"

"I haven't the slightest idea. She's very attractive, though."

"In that calculating I-eat-minions-for-lunch kind of way," he said, which brought a smile to Skylar's lips. His observation was true. The woman's lips were the color of fresh blood, and she wore her hair in a severe wedge of glossy black that resembled a helmet.

Cole sat back and studied her for a minute. "Why are you nervous about the guy?"

"I'm not."

"Yes, you are."

"Okay, I am," she said, not sure what to add. She wasn't a child and she didn't need to ask permission to leave the mansion, yet there was no denying she hadn't told her uncle her plans for the simple reason she had the weird feeling he would ask her not to go until his check was complete, and she didn't want to openly defy him. He was unfailingly kind to her, but he was also a man of determination and power, and at times, she thought he might even be a little on the autocratic side.

But how did she tell the confident, self-assured guy sitting across from her that she didn't want her uncle's secretary blabbing her private business? She would sound like an idiot. "I get the feeling he's a bit of a gossip," she said, settling on an abbreviated version of the truth.

"You don't want him telling your uncle he saw you here with me," Cole said.

"You have to understand…it's hard enough living in the house with protective relatives without giving them every detail of your life."

"I can only imagine," he said. "Do you want to leave?"

She shook her head. "I don't think he saw me, and even if he did, I'm not sure he would recognize me. I only know him because I saw a picture of him with Uncle Luca in the newspaper one day, and the caption identified him."

"Your uncle doesn't invite him to his home?"

"No. He says he likes to keep business and home life separate from each other."

"I didn't think politicians had that luxury."

She shrugged. "I don't know. He told me once that letting underlings get too close could be dangerous—that he had firsthand experience with the fact that men in his profession could stab you in the back while they smiled in your face."

Cole's amazing blue eyes seemed to darken, or maybe it was just his expression. Maybe it was neither; maybe it was her imagination. "He sounds cautious," he said at last.

"You have no idea." She took a deep breath and a sip of wine. "Let's pretend Ian isn't here. It's not the end of the world if he sees me, anyway."

"I wonder if the woman works with your uncle, too."

"I have no idea."

He opened his mouth again, then closed it without speaking, leaving something unsaid, but what, she had no inkling. Seeking to change the subject, she speared a clam and asked, "Do you really live in Vegas?"

"I really do."

"Do you go to the casinos all the time?"

"Rarely," he said, twisting linguine on his fork.

"You don't care for games of chance?"

"Not that kind," he said, smiling that way he had that seemed to impart a whole other layer of meaning to his words.

They fell silent while they finished dinner. Skylar was sure Ian Banderas hadn't yet noticed her, and she was anxious to leave but swallowed her impatience when the waiter showed up with a dessert tray and Cole asked her if she'd like to split something over coffee.

The tiramisu arrived with coffee strong enough to fuel the whole town for an hour or two. Skylar forgot all about Ian as she and Cole scooted closer together in order to share dessert. Their confidences grew a little more intimate as they discussed past relationships and future dreams, and her head swam with compliments as he admired the dress she'd created and worn that evening: a short sheath made up of a half-dozen different black fabrics including lace and satin and velvet with a few iridescent feathers just for fun.

They were in the process of polishing off their last sips of coffee when a woman came into the emptying dining room. She caught Skylar's attention because of the furtive way she looked around and because her inexpensive clothes were so outdated and worn. She was unaccompanied as she stood near the door and searched the room, and then it seemed to Skylar that their gazes met. The woman started toward their table, sending waves of anxiety ahead of her that seemed to ripple through the air like something tangible and concrete.

Skylar put her cup down so fast it rattled on its saucer. Cole looked up. He apparently discerned the same feelings of uneasiness that Skylar had. He squeezed her hand and then stood as if providing a barrier, but the woman didn't even pause as she moved right past them both. Instead, she came to a halt at the table of Banderas and his dinner companion. Cole sat down again, his gaze connecting with Skylar's.

Standing over Ian, the woman spoke in a breathless, anxiety-ridden tone that was so soft only the emotion came through loud and clear. Cole sat back down and met Skylar's gaze. When he opened his mouth as if to inquire what was going on, she shook her head, straining to hear what was being said.

But it was almost hopeless. The words were spoken so softly and with such distress and urgency they blended together like an off-key song. A few words stood out, but mostly it seemed like pleading and begging with flashes of fear thrown in.

Management showed up in the form of a tuxedo-wearing maître d' with a pencil-thin mustache. Skylar turned in her chair to glimpse the man stopping beside the woman and speaking briefly with her. The woman looked trapped as she peered around the room, then the maître d' clutched her arm and ushered her away. Her soft cries haunted Skylar as she departed—another sad, mournful event in a day that seemed destined to end in tragedy of one kind or another.

Skylar's gaze swiveled back to Ian, who had taken out his phone. Before she could look away, he'd risen to his feet and sped past her, talking hurriedly as he moved. He took the street entrance and disappeared into the night. The woman he'd been dining with took out a credit card and signaled their waiter.

"I guess the floor show is over," Cole said.

"I guess so," Skylar said, turning to face him. "I wonder what that was all about?"

"You couldn't tell?"

"No. They spoke too softly. It sounded like she was pleading for her life."

"I obviously couldn't understand her, but her manner triumphed over language barriers," Cole said. "She was terrified."

"Yeah."

He signed the check, then helped Skylar with her coat, and they left the restaurant, exiting into the lobby. They paused behind a trio of potted palms. "Will you come up to my room?" he asked quietly, gazing down into her eyes.

She wanted to. She wanted to forget about Aneta's blood and the forlorn woman's begging, forget about sadness and doubt....

But then she remembered the kiss with which Cole had greeted her that evening and the resulting flare of passion and desire. All evening their gazes had locked as they ate and chatted and danced around the flaming heat that seemed to unite them. She shook her head. "I can't."

"Pity," he said, his hand resting lightly on her shoulder, his gaze consuming her.

"You may not believe me," she added, "but normally I don't kiss men I just meet."

"I hope not," he said.

"Well, I could see how you might get the impression..." Her voice trailed off as she realized she'd painted herself into a corner.

He smiled. "Don't worry, Skylar. It never crossed my mind."

"I don't know why it wouldn't," she said. "I haven't exactly been pushing you away."

His smile turned speculative. "You don't honestly think I go around kissing every pretty girl who will let me, do you?"

"Don't you?"

"Hell, no."

"But—"

"*But* you're different," he said. "Today has been different. Accelerated, kind of. Do you know what I mean?"

"Yes."

"Right from the start," he added, and the way his voice dipped and his eyes burned into her made her reconsider his offer.

"I'll call you a cab," he said, and releasing her shoulder, he walked over to the desk and put in a request. When he returned, he took her hand and walked out to the curb with her. The cab arrived within minutes, and he opened the back door, ushered her inside and then followed.

"What are you doing?" she asked.

"Seeing you home. I'll take the taxi back to the hotel."

"That's not necessary—"

"Why don't you tell the cabbie where you live?" he said, the smile back.

After she leaned forward to give the man her address, she sat back against the seat and turned her head to look up at Cole's dark profile. "It's been a lovely evening," she said. "I'm glad I came."

"I'm glad you came, too."

"My uncle's estate isn't far. We should be there within minutes."

His fingers brushed her face, tilting her chin up, his lips so close she felt them move when he spoke. "Then we better start saying goodbye right now," he said. The heat of his breath made her quiver as his mouth closed over hers.

COLE RETURNED TO HIS ROOM a little uneasy about the evening. Where had his noble intentions gone? How could he justify finding out the truth and exacting justice for

himself while taking those very things away from someone else?

Especially from someone he was beginning to care
about?

Not that kissing Skylar had been anything but genuine on his part. Who wouldn't want to kiss her? But his
motives were complicated—even to him—and he knew
if he was honest with her about his intentions and goals,
she would be as likely to push him under a bus as ever
look at him again. And he couldn't chance losing her because then he would be worse off than before, his very
presence a red flag to Luca Futura. At that point, his best
bet would be to get out of Kanistan as quickly as possible.

There was a saying his adoptive father had uttered at
times: in for a penny, in for a pound.

As he unlocked his room door with the swipe of a
card, he wondered again about Ian Banderas and the sad
woman who had come up to him in the public venue of a
restaurant. From her demeanor, it was obvious she wasn't
the kind to cause a stir, which in itself underlined a des-
peration to her action. Skylar had picked up on it immediately as had he.

The door closed behind him, and he paused for a second, reviewing, in his mind's eye, the sight of Skylar
seated across from him, her expression as soft as her lips,
her eyes glowing in the candlelight, so young and pretty
and such a world away from anyone and anything he'd
ever experienced that he felt as drawn to her, in his way,
as that woman had been drawn to Ian Banderas.

But there had been a somber note to their parting that
had been unexpected. At first he thought the hurried way
she left the cab had to do with the accumulation of too
many unexpected and overwhelming events of the day,
but on the way back, he'd speculated it might be that he

was rushing her. Hadn't she mentioned him going fast the minute he kissed her?

He took a deep breath and, out of habit, checked the small case he kept atop the dresser, positioned just so with the image of a compass on top pointing one degree south of northwest.

It was off by that one degree. Someone had made it line up just right, which meant it was wrong.

And that meant someone had been in the room.

His gaze swiveled to the bed, which was turned down with a candy on the pillow just as it had been the night before. The maid had been here. She could have been intrigued by the case and tried to open it. Hell, she could have set something down on the dresser that scooted it out of position. Time to check the other safeguard—this one the felt bag he kept in the back of the bottom drawer.

The bag was where it was supposed to be, and he retrieved it, carrying it to the bed where he sat down to examine the loose knot in the beige cord. It looked exactly as it had when he left except that the extra beige thread that he habitually threaded in the knot was missing. Someone had untied the cord to uncover a wad of euros folded inside. As he expected, the money was intact…and that meant his searcher hadn't been a thief. He'd been after something else.

Who else but Luca Futura or, more accurately, one of his henchmen?

The question was simple: Did they find anything to arouse suspicion? Doubtful. He had a briefcase full of documents for a legitimate business that he'd bought into the week before coming here. His ID would reveal he was exactly who he said he was, because for all intents and purposes, he *was* exactly who he said he was.

Maybe this was business as usual for a man like Futura,

who would be speculative about anyone who crossed his path no matter how peripherally. But how did they know Cole would be out of his room?

Two possibilities: it was no coincidence that Ian Banderas had been in the dining room because he'd come here at Futura's bidding, *or* Skylar Pope's arrival hadn't been as innocent as it appeared.

Was that possible? He couldn't imagine there was a duplicitous bone in her body, yet the way she'd said goodnight when they arrived at the palatial estate of her aunt and uncle had held a note of finality, leaving him wondering if the dinner invitation would ultimately be rescinded and Skylar would disappear from his reach. Maybe her uncle had given her the task of distracting him.

He shook his head at his own paranoia then, remembering the clown, he crossed the room to open the drawer. The clown was where he'd left it. What had the searcher made of a grown man carrying around an obviously old toy like this?

More importantly, if whoever had searched this room reported the presence of the clown to Luca Futura, would it raise an alarm in the man's distant memory?

Well, he'd know tomorrow night if not sooner.

Chapter Five

The next day, assuming he was being watched in some capacity, Cole went through the motions of visiting different outlets, placing orders and discussing sales with contacts his new partner had made in the months before. Those contacts and the partner's floundering ability to pay his overhead were the reasons Cole had bought into Nevada Consolidated in the first place. He now owned four-fifths of a company teetering on the edge of bankruptcy, and the truth of the matter was that it would probably go under and he would lose every penny.

But that was just money. What he had needed was the legitimacy of a career change after his injuries had forced him out of the army. When Luca Futura researched Cole Bennett, he mustn't find anything to arouse suspicion.

Half expecting a call that canceled dinner plans, Cole checked his room messages often throughout the day. The call never came, and at seven, warned by the concierge the city's maze of streets wasn't to be tackled lightly by foreigners after dark, he showed up at Futura's front gate in a taxi and was ushered inside by a very proper-looking butler with a British accent.

Skylar abandoned her seat on a brocaded sofa and approached him. He had to remind himself to breathe. She was dressed in what surely must be one of her creations, an artless dress composed of many different patterns of fabric that fell from her slender shoulders and stopped just above her knees. The streak in her hair was now more purple than pink, and the smile she wore lit up the high-ceilinged room.

One thing Skylar wasn't was a chameleon. She did not blend in to her surroundings. Take this room, all gilded and glitzy and full of antiques he hoped no one would think to ask him about. Skylar didn't clash with it exactly; she just had such a strong sense of style and of herself that she remained undiminished, just as she had in Aneta's apartment building the day before.

He tore his gaze from her dazzling face to see another woman, this one older and frailer. She, too, sat on the sofa, a blue scarf wrapped around what must be thinning hair, her skin translucent. It was obvious she'd lost weight recently, but he found the same spirit in her eyes that he found in Skylar's, and her handshake upon introduction was welcoming.

"I am so very pleased to meet you," Skylar's aunt said, her voice gentle. "Please forgive my husband," she added. "He's busy putting out fires over the phone, but he'll be downstairs in a moment. Can we get you something to drink?"

"Whatever you're having would be fine," Cole said, glancing at the cup that sat before her on a low coffee table.

"I can't drink alcohol right now," she said. "This is just herbal tea. I'd like to offer something more exciting to the man who did so much for Skylar yesterday and tried to help poor Aneta. Skylar, ask Davis to pour wine."

"Only if Skylar will join me," Cole said.

"Of course I will," Skylar said, and actually pulled on a cord just as he'd seen people do in movies. Within seconds, the butler showed up and opened a bottle of wine, delivering two glasses before departing.

"I'm very sorry about your employee, Ms. Ables. If we'd only arrived a few minutes sooner, maybe we could have made a difference."

"Or maybe you both would have been hurt, as well. There's no use in thinking what if, is there?"

"Have the police any leads on the theft or the murder?" Cole asked.

"I'm not sure," Skylar said. "I was at the shop all day trying to figure out if anything else is missing."

"What would I do without you?" her aunt asked with an affectionate smile.

Skylar smiled back. "You know I love to help you out, Aunt Eleanor."

"And *is* anything else missing?" Cole asked.

"I don't believe so, but I've suggested to Aunt Eleanor that she have an auditor look through the books to be on the safe side."

"I think it's a good idea," Eleanor said.

"This is quite a house," Cole said after a short lull, uncomfortable with his own prying questions.

"I think it's rather ostentatious," Eleanor said, her eyes lively. "But my husband loves it."

"Has it been in his family for generations?" he asked.

"Oh, no. No, his parents were humble people of limited means. But Luca worked for an American ambassador way back when, and after the explosion that killed the man and his family, Luca was called to fill increasingly demanding roles."

"An explosion? Here in Traterg?"

"Yes. We had just married. Kanistan was very strange to me at first. So political. The country was uneasy, so I guess it was natural that I would become friendly with the only other American woman I knew, and that was Ambassador Oates's wife, Mary."

"Was the American ambassador's death political in nature?" Cole asked, trying to keep the anxiousness out of his voice.

"No, I'm afraid it wasn't. My husband doesn't like to talk about it, but it seems the ambassador had an affair with a much younger woman. Lenora Roman was her name. Mind you, I found this so hard to believe. I'd met him several times when I visited them with Luca, and the ambassador always seemed like such a decent man. Anyway, Lenora became pregnant, and then she was murdered. The police discovered that her father and brothers assumed it was the ambassador's doing and sent a bomb to the house in retaliation. The blast destroyed the whole family."

"There were no survivors?"

She shook her head. "No. They all died. The ambassador, Mary and worst of all his son by a first marriage and the two smaller boys he and Mary had together. My husband was just devastated."

"Now, Eleanor," a voice said from behind Cole, who jerked in surprise. He'd been totally wound up in Eleanor's story and hadn't heard Luca Futura enter the room.

Cole rose to his feet to greet his host and found the man's distant smile in place.

"I'm sorry, Luca," Eleanor said. "I don't know what got into me talking about all that. I know you don't like to remember any of it."

Luca leaned down and kissed his wife's head. "No worries, my darling," he said. No, he didn't say it, he sang it, his voice trailing off into a melody.

Cole sat down so abruptly that the other three looked

up at him. "I'm sorry," he said, feeling exposed. He had the irrational desire to leave the house immediately.

"What's wrong?" Skylar asked.

"I tripped on my own feet," he said, trying out a self-deprecating laugh.

Luca smiled. "You do not strike me as a clumsy man," he said.

"I'm usually not," Cole said. "That was a pretty tune you hummed a minute ago."

"It's a folk song. Not many people know it anymore, but it still plays on in my mind."

Eleanor began singing, her voice a little reedy, and that somehow made the lyrics more poignant. "No worries, my darling, I'll always be near. No worries forever, just sleep. Tomorrow will dawn with the sun bright and clear. No worries, my darling, just sleep." She looked up at her husband, and he squeezed her hand. Then she looked at Cole and added, "Luca used to sing that song to Skylar when she was little. Remember, Luca?"

"Yes, I remember," he said.

Skylar rose and poured her uncle a glass of wine. She handed it to him, and he sat beside his wife while Skylar took a chair so close to Cole he could reach out and touch her. And that's exactly what he wanted to do. He wanted to get her alone, away from that house, away from the images her aunt had just planted in his head right before her husband had hummed a tune.

He also wanted to tell Eleanor how much he appreciated the tree-of-life paperweight Skylar had given him but hesitated, unsure if her uncle knew that she'd seen him the night before and not sure if the news would be welcome. It was impossible to miss his protective vibe. Instead, Cole talked about Eleanor's exhibit at the gallery and how much he had enjoyed that, although the truth was that it was almost impossible to connect this delicate woman with the powerhouse artist she must really be.

"That endeavor was a labor of love for me," she said, obviously pleased with his compliments. "When I'm better, I plan to start a new project. This time I want to do volcanoes of the Pacific Rim, like Krakatoa and Pinatubo, and even Mount St. Helens in the Pacific Northwest."

"I can see I'm going to have to start a collection," Cole said.

"Perhaps you should ask Mr. Bennett about the table in the drawing room," Luca said, addressing his wife. "I imagine he could settle its origins once and for all. He must know a lot about antiques."

"I'm afraid that's not true," Cole said. "I'm new to this."

"What do you mean?" Skylar asked.

"I recently bought into an acquaintance's business. I was injured overseas, while serving," he explained to the others. "After I recovered, I needed a new direction, and Martin needed a partner. Right now I'm just learning as I go."

The butler showed up to announce dinner, and they retired to the dining room, another over-the-top area. Eleanor, as expected, barely touched her meal, and Skylar seemed intent on keeping a light conversation going. Luca appeared content to sit back and watch their interaction.

The goal had been to get close to Luca and find out the truth of that thirty-year-old explosion, but now that he'd wormed his way into the house, Cole wasn't sure how to proceed. Maybe reminding the man of the one slim bond they'd forged would help. He waited until dinner was almost finished before broaching the subject of Aneta Cazo's murder, asking once again about leads.

"I hear they have one," Luca said, setting his napkin aside.

"Can you share the details?"

"There aren't many," he said with an elegant shrug, "and none I would care to discuss in front of my wife and niece."

"Your wife is tired," Eleanor said, folding her napkin. Her voice did sound strained, suggesting that maybe she was in pain. "It's time for me to retire."

"I've overstayed," Cole began, but she cut him off.

"Nonsense. It's this damn disease, or maybe the treatment is even worse. Stay and talk to Luca."

"Let me summon your nurse," Futura said.

"That's not necessary. Skylar will help me upstairs. Won't you, dear? And once again, thank you, Cole, for your support yesterday."

"I was happy to be of service," he said, and watched as Skylar ushered her aunt from the room.

"Let's adjourn to my den," Luca said. "I have a bottle of excellent French brandy."

"Thanks," Cole said and fought the impulse to bus his place at the table. All these servants and fancy sauces were a little tricky for a guy who was still more accustomed to eating MREs in a trench.

They were crossing the foyer when a loud knock sounded and the butler showed up. He ushered in a slightly built man with slick blond hair that looked damp—it must have started raining. The man took off his coat and all but threw it at the butler. Ignoring Cole, he made straight for Luca, who towered over him.

Ian Banderas in the pale flesh, and mad as a hornet, as well.

He spoke rapidly and in a language Cole understood three words of: hello, goodbye and please. As far as he could tell, Banderas didn't say a single one of those words.

Futura scowled at Ian in response. In fact, it looked as

if the older man wanted to pitch Banderas out altogether. Instead, he spoke to the butler, who led Banderas away toward what Cole assumed was the den.

Futura turned back to Cole and spread his hands. "I am very sorry, Mr. Bennett. This situation demands my attention. My associate should never have come here, but now that he has—well, suffice to say I will have to terminate our evening without the brandy. Perhaps if business brings you back to Traterg, you will look us up. Until then, good night."

The butler was back with Cole's coat in hand, leaving Cole with little choice but to gracefully make his exit.

He stood outside the door under the portico as the rain drummed overhead, contemplating walking back to the hotel in the rain or calling a cab. Luca must have been more upset than he let on to dismiss a guest without asking if he needed help. Not that Cole did. It was just a little over four miles and the walk, wet or not, would do him good.

What really kept him standing there was the fact that he had hardly spoken to Skylar. She'd been polite that evening but nothing more, the kisses and growing intimacy of the night before missing as though they'd never happened. He shouldn't care. He'd used her to get in the front door, and while there was still need for a return visit, he could think of another strategy if he had to.

What bothered him was the concern he'd said or done something the night before that had alerted her to his secret mission. What if she said something to her uncle? That was the problem, right? Not that he wanted more of her, just that she might jeopardize what he had to do.

So why did her demeanor that evening leave him feeling alone? He hardly ever felt that way—not as an only kid growing up or as a soldier with his own agenda or during the months of hospital care and recuperation for his injured leg. Vulnerability was a luxury he couldn't afford. Never had.

He stepped into the rain and started down the curving drive until he heard his name called and turned. Skylar stood under the portico now, her fair hair gleaming in the overhead light. As he stood staring at her, she dashed out to meet him.

"You left without saying goodbye," she said.

"Your uncle had a guest. And truthfully, I didn't know if you'd care. You were so formal tonight."

"It's that house," she said, hugging herself. "It gets to me. Normally it's okay, but seeing you there just felt weird and watching my aunt struggle to act normal was painful. She and my uncle try so hard to pretend nothing is wrong."

"Is her prognosis good?"

"Yes. If she can survive the treatments, she should recover. She's just worn out."

"I shouldn't have come," he said, feeling like the lowest bug on earth.

"No, that's why she wanted me to go upstairs with her, so she could tell me how nice she thought you were. She enjoyed meeting you. It's just me being a worrywart. I'm sorry."

"You don't have to be sorry." He brushed wet hair away from her forehead. "You're getting all wet."

"I don't care. It feels great out here."

"It's kind of cold. Where's your coat?"

"I didn't want to take time to find it. I just wanted to say good-night."

He'd waited long enough that evening, and unbuttoning his cashmere overcoat, he shrugged it off and draped it over her shoulders, then pulled her against him. He kissed her the way he'd wanted to all night as cold drops hit their heads and rolled down their faces. The icy water juxtaposed with the heat of their mouths translated into the sexiest kiss he'd ever experienced. He lost himself for a second in the moist softness of her mouth and the feel of her breasts pressed against his chest.

She pulled away at last and looked back toward the house. "Not here," she said.

"Then come back to the hotel with me."

"I shouldn't," she said, turning to look back at the house.

"Yes," he said firmly. "You should. You must."

"But—"

"No buts. No arguments. Just come."

Her smile was slow and sexy, and the water drenching her hair just made her look more desirable. "Do you always get your way?"

"I'm not going to answer that," he said, kissing her forehead and eyelids.

"Why not?"

"Because if I say I do you might feel it necessary to teach me a lesson, and if I say I don't you might feel sorry for me and sympathy is the last thing I want from you."

Her voice so low it was hard to hear, she said, "What do you want from me?"

"Nothing," he said. "Everything."

She was quiet for a second, and the only discernable noise was the rain hitting the pavement. "Cole, is there something you're not telling me?"

He froze for an instant. What had she seen or heard that alerted her he was more—and less—than he presented himself to be? He kissed her forehead and said, "What do you mean?"

"Oh, I don't know," she said, and he could tell she was dismissing her own suspicions, ignoring her instincts. He wasn't very happy with himself and decided for both their sakes this evening should come to an end.

And then she said, "I'll go get my aunt's car and give you a lift back to the hotel. I can't imagine why my uncle didn't call you a cab. Meet me at the gatehouse."

She left without waiting for a response, his long coat flopping around her legs as she ran. He dashed toward the street and the protective arch that spanned the driveway, connecting the gatehouse with an eight-foot-high stone wall that he knew from satellite pictures surrounded the property.

He stared back at the house, waiting for Skylar's headlights, wondering if she'd leave word for her uncle where she was going and what Futura would make of that. If it offended him that Cole was seeing his niece, would it jeopardize his standing with the man?

And what about Skylar?

This wasn't fair to her. It wasn't in the plans for him to develop feelings for her. At first he'd thought their mutual attraction might be a bonus, but now it presented itself as a pit of vipers.

He heard a noise behind him, from the street side of the arch, and turned, wondering how Skylar had arrived from that direction. He sensed movement, and then something very hard smashed against his head and he fell to the ground, landing first on his hands and knees and then facedown, his cheek in a puddle. He heard a gasp as lights appeared from somewhere. He saw a leg close by and grabbed it down around the ankle. The black skin pulled away from the bone. Stockings. The person the leg was connected to made a grunting noise and tried to pull free, but even though Cole's head filled with blurred stars, he held on tight.

He heard other sounds he couldn't place. More voices,

one of them Skylar's, but the words were incomprehensible. His grip lessened until his attacker yanked free. Cole tried to tell Skylar to run, but his lips wouldn't move.

His attacker fell down to the ground next to him, sobbing.

He looked up, but her face was covered with her hands. Above her he glimpsed Skylar, eyes wide with shock. And then he saw nothing.

Chapter Six

Skylar wasn't sure what to do. Cole appeared to be out cold, and his attacker had dissolved into tears mumbling over and over again, "God forgive me, I killed the wrong man." Not that Skylar figured that out all at once. The tears garbled the crying woman's voice; it was only through repetition that Skylar finally understood what she was saying.

"You didn't kill him," Skylar said, though she'd seen the wooden bat the woman must have clobbered Cole with, and the fact he was alive seemed like a miracle.

The woman suddenly looked up toward the house. Her tone changed from remorse to fear. "He's still here! You are friends of his?"

"Friends of who?"

"That man. He took my little girl."

"What man?" Skylar demanded. "Who are you talking about?"

"Banderas," she said, spitting the name as though it left a bad taste in her mouth. "How many more must he take?"

"You're the woman from the hotel restaurant," Skylar said, finally recognizing her. "What's your name?"

"Svetlana Dacho. Do you know where he took Malina?"

"Listen, ma'am. I'm sorry, but you have the wrong house. My aunt and uncle live here."

The woman shook Cole's arm. "Maybe he knows."

"Leave him alone. You've done enough."

"Skylar?"

She looked down at Cole, trying to shield his face from the rain with her back, pulling the frantic woman's hands away from Cole. "Oh my gosh, Cole, thank goodness. Are you okay?"

Thanks to the headlights on her aunt's car, she could see him try to focus his gaze on her face. His hand slowly went to the back of his head and he winced. "I don't know," he muttered, his words broken. "I think so. Was I out long?"

"No, just a few seconds."

His attention traveled to the woman who had attacked him. "Is that—"

"The woman from the restaurant last night? Yes."

"Why did she hit me?"

"I don't think she meant to hit you. I think she meant to hit someone else."

"Ian Banderas," he mumbled, trying to sit.

At the mention of the Banderas name, the woman sat back, and her sobs abated. "You know that slime? He left money as though he could buy my silence. Where did he take her?"

Cole, of course, didn't understand a word of this and looked at Skylar for help. "She's convinced Ian Banderas is here at the house and apparently has something to do with the disappearance of her daughter."

"She's right," he said, trying to sit. "Banderas is here."

The woman seemed to sense that Skylar and Cole couldn't or wouldn't help her, for she stood suddenly, the bat back in her hand. Skylar rose to protect Cole from another attack, but it wasn't necessary. Without another word, the woman turned and ran toward the street, disappearing into the shadows and the rainy night.

Skylar looked down at Cole, who had managed to sit. He was rubbing his neck as rain flattened his hair to his head. He looked bedraggled but undefeated as he asked her for a hand.

"Ian Banderas isn't here," she said, pulling him to his feet. "I'll help you back up to the house."

"No."

"Cole, really. We'll get my aunt's nurse to take a look at you."

"Not necessary," he said.

"Yes, it is."

"This is nothing," he said, fighting a losing battle with brushing mud off his suit. "I've had a lot worse. All I need is my own bed…and an aspirin." He looked down at the ground as though it hurt to raise his head. "Will you drive me back to the hotel?"

"Of course I will."

She helped him around to the passenger door, and he got in with a grunt. "Good thing the seats are leather. I'm a little damp."

"Don't worry about it."

She closed his door and walked around the car. His coat had kept her body dry and warm, but the wool garment was soaked now and heavy and made slipping behind the wheel a bit tricky. Her hair was as wet as Cole's, and she turned the heater up and glanced over at him.

His head rested against the seat, eyes closed. "Let's go before someone comes outside to see what's going on," he said as though sensing her looking at him.

"Why? You've done nothing wrong."

"I know, but I have a funny feeling that Banderas has."

"My uncle would never employ a dishonest man."

"Skylar? Could we just go?"

She started the car's engine and turned out onto the street. There was no sign of the woman. "What do you mean Ian Banderas is here?"

"He came to see your uncle."

"He never comes to the house."

"I got the feeling your uncle wasn't too happy about it. Banderas seemed agitated."

"Maybe he knew that woman was trailing him."

His eyes still closed, he shook his head and groaned. "Ouch. No, I don't think Banderas is the kind of guy to let a middle-aged woman scare him. But I didn't see a car. He must have taken a cab, and if he did, how did she manage to follow him on foot?"

"My uncle's office is across the street and around the corner from the estate," she said. "Ian probably walked over."

Cole's eyes fluttered open. "Do you suppose the woman's situation is connected to Aneta's murder?"

This time, Skylar shook her head. "I don't know. It's hard to imagine how. I hardly think you chased a middle-aged woman down the fire escape and mistook her for a guy."

"No, it was a man, I'm sure of that. What kind of car does Banderas drive?"

"I have no idea, but really, Cole, don't be absurd. My uncle is a very astute man. If Ian was doing something shady, he would know."

"Why else would that woman be hell-bent on bonking him?"

"I don't know, but just because she's under the impression Ian has something to do with her daughter's apparent disappearance doesn't mean it's true."

"Yeah," he said, but he didn't sound convinced.

"Did my uncle tell you about the police lead he mentioned at dinner?"

"Banderas arrived before he could say anything. Do you know what he was alluding to?"

"No clue." She was silent for a moment and then commented, "Your hotel is up ahead."

"You can let me off at the front."

"No, I'm going to make sure you get tucked in all safe and sound," she said.

She could feel him gazing at her. She guessed he wasn't particularly fond of needing help, but that was too bad. She'd let him get away without seeing the nurse, but she wasn't dropping him off at the hotel entrance.

It was still relatively early, and their wet, disheveled state raised eyebrows from the parking valet to the lobby staff. Cole's limp was more pronounced than ever as they made their way down the long hallway to his room.

Once inside, she shooed him into the bathroom with directions to take a hot shower. He handed her out his suit, and she deposited it and his overcoat into dry cleaning bags and called housekeeping to pick them up outside the room. Then she called through the bathroom door, asking Cole if he had aspirin, and he told her he'd already used a glass of tap water to take two from the bottle he carried in his shaving kit.

As he bathed, she used the brush in her purse to comb out her damp hair, then started opening drawers, looking for pajamas for him. The first drawer she opened revealed the box she'd given him the night before and also a colorful figurine of a clown that looked old and worn. She picked up the figurine, too curious to mind her own business.

Why did a guy like Cole Bennett carry around a child's

toy? It added an unexpected dimension to him, another little puzzling thing that she couldn't identify or stick with a label, just as his watchful demeanor that night had made her wonder if he was there for a reason he wasn't sharing.

"Please put that down," he said, and she whirled around guiltily, the clown still in her hand. He stood just inside the room, a white towel wrapped around his waist. His exposed skin glistened with dampness, the muscles beneath chiseled and defined. She'd known he was put together better than your average male, but the true extent of his fitness left her shaky.

She turned back around and replaced the clown. Raising her gaze, she saw in the mirror that he was now standing right behind her, his reflected image intent on what she was doing. The man moved like a cat, limp and all.

She closed the drawer and turned again, ending up right against him. She was as aware of the towel knotted at his waist as she was the clean, fresh scent of his newly washed skin.

"I wasn't prying," she said. "I was looking for your pajamas."

He smiled that way he had. "I don't wear pajamas."

Of course he didn't.

He took her hand and led her toward the bed.

"How's your head?" she asked.

"Nothing an old soldier can't handle," he said and sat down. As the towel rode up his muscular thighs, she got a glimpse of his left knee and swallowed a gasp.

His gaze followed the direction of her own. "Sit down," he said gently.

She sat down beside him. "Does it hurt?"

"My knee? Yeah, at times. I must have fallen on it tonight."

It was obvious he'd had more than one operation and

also that it was relatively new as the scars hadn't entirely healed. She touched the surrounding skin, and he flinched. She got the feeling it wasn't because she'd hurt him but because she'd actually touched him.

He raised her chin with his fingertips. "I took a piece of shrapnel in Afghanistan."

"I'm so sorry."

"I got out alive. The others weren't so lucky, so all and all, a limp is a small price to pay."

"And it cut your career short?"

"I could have stayed on and done other kinds of work, but that wasn't what I wanted. By the time I got out of rehab, I was finished with that part of my life. Now you know the whole story."

She doubted it. He was glossing over the physical and emotional pain he must have experienced, but she understood his instinct to protect himself.

"I'll turn my back, and you can get under the covers," she said, trying not to imagine what he would look like when that towel fell to the floor.

"You don't have to turn your back," he said, his mouth very close to hers.

"You have a head injury," she whispered.

He glanced down at his lap, and her gaze followed. It was obvious his body was responding with a mind of its own, and she yearned to touch the growing shape, strip away the towel, feast her eyes on him, feel her against him and inside of her. She licked her lips.

"You smell wonderful," he said, nuzzling her neck. His breath was hot against her skin as his hands slid around her back. She leaned into him. His mouth closed over hers, and she felt like she was drowning, sensations coming over her like waves she couldn't climb. The kisses grew deeper, one hand buried in her hair, the other caressing her neck.

Her uncle never would have admitted Cole into his home if Cole hadn't checked out to be who and what he said he was. But that kind of check didn't address a person's character directly; only time and experience would reveal those traits.

Did she care? Right this second? Um, no.

He pulled her back on the bed and half covered her with his hard, lean body. As he kissed her over and over, deeper and harder, his hands roamed her chest, and though no buttons were undone or straps removed, her flesh felt almost naked under the heat of his fingers. He pulled her against him and delivered the granddaddy of kisses while his hand caught the bare flesh of her thigh, and she knew it was time to shed her clothes. Instead, he caught her shoulders and sat up, pulling her with him, holding her so tight against his chest she couldn't breathe and she didn't care. When he looked down at her, she stared back, lips parted, eyes half closed. He looked as frazzled as she felt.

"Skylar? This isn't a good idea," he whispered.

She wanted only to wrap her arms around his solid torso. She was hot and moist and feeling almost drunk with desire. What was his problem? "But—"

"No," he said, gently, settling a fingertip against her lips. She could feel a tremor in his hand as though he was fighting a great battle.

"Is it your head?" she said, coming back to her senses.

He continued to stare at her, and then he nodded. "Yes. It's my head."

"Of course," she said. "I should have thought of that. Let me look."

"No, it's okay."

"Lower your head," she demanded, and he finally did.

She carefully parted his soft dark hair. The skin was a little swollen and red but not broken. "Does it hurt?"

"Yes."

"And you're sure about not seeing a doctor?"

"Absolutely." He got to his feet and so did she, demurely turning her back while he dropped the towel and slid between the sheets. He yawned and settled into his pillow. "I just need to sleep," he said.

She'd never known it was possible for a guy to go from hot and breathing heavy to sleepy that fast. Either she was the most boring lover the world had ever known or he truly did hurt.

"Good night," she said. She took a card from her wallet and set it beside his lamp. "That's my phone number. Don't hesitate to call if you need something."

"Will I see you tomorrow?" he asked, gazing up at her as she switched off his lamp.

She leaned down and kissed his forehead. "That's up to you. Call me."

He caught her hand, then released it. Using the light from the bathroom to navigate, she let herself out of his room.

HE LAY THERE FOR QUITE A WHILE thinking he'd never get to sleep, trying to figure out the identity and significance of the woman who had hit him and what her problem was. Skylar hadn't said much, and what she had said was kind of lost in the quicksand of his near concussion. Something about Banderas taking her daughter.

Was it possible Futura was involved in some kind of human trafficking? Look at what he'd done decades earlier; this wasn't such a big stretch for a man who forged passports and adoption papers.

Maybe Ian was Futura's partner in crime. Maybe the woman was trying to bash the wrong man.

If this was true, where did it leave Skylar? Now his thoughts flew back to her, and he took a deep breath. He had won a few medals for bravery and things like that, but the real medals should come for doing the decent thing and not making love to a woman who (a) he wanted and (b) wanted him. She'd been his for the taking, and instead, he'd put her back on the shelf, neat as a pin and undamaged to boot.

He must have slept because eventually he awoke to a ringing phone. He sat up too fast, and the room took a spin. He grasped his forehead with both hands. As he sat there contemplating moving again, the hotel phone went silent. He eventually managed to get both feet on the floor and shuffle into the bathroom where he took another shower and two more aspirin. A new towel fastened around his waist, he was in the process of leaving the bathroom when the phone rang again and he snagged the receiver.

"This is Cole," he said, expecting to hear Skylar's warm voice.

Instead he heard the crisp words of a woman he didn't recognize. Her English was excellent but accented. "I am Irina Churo. Your brother gave me your number."

His brother.

The concept still amazed him. And not just one brother—two. After growing up an only child, he found it a pretty incredible experience to suddenly have a family. Not that he could mention their existence to anyone, not until this mess in Kanistan was cleared up, but the knowledge they were back home waiting for him was like the promise of a fire in the hearth when you're slogging through the snow. "You're talking about John?" he said. His other brother, Tyler, had never been to Kanistan.

"Yes. He mentioned me, perhaps?"

"Yes, Irina, he did. You're a policewoman in Slovo. John met you months ago when he came to Kanistan to investigate his memory loss."

"Yes, and again when he was trying to find his brothers. I called him recently with news, and he asked that I contact you because you are here in Kanistan. Would it be possible for you to travel to Slovo, say tomorrow?"

"Is it important?" he asked and then regretted it. John wouldn't have given this woman his number if he didn't trust her and if what she'd told him hadn't struck him that her information would help. Before she could answer, he inserted, "Never mind. Should I call this number when I get there or drop in at the police station?"

"Oh, no," she said quickly, her voice dropping in volume. "No. Before you get to town, there's a bridge with green turrets. You can't miss it. There's a building on the bridge. I will meet you there after work, say, four o'clock in the afternoon."

"All right," he said. "How will I know you?"

"I'll wear a black coat over my uniform and a green scarf. Perhaps you could carry something."

He felt as though he'd just wandered into an old spy thriller! "Not necessary," he said. "Just look for a man with a limp."

"I see. Until tomorrow, then."

He hung up the phone and called Skylar, disappointed when it went to her voice mail. Headache now superseded by hunger, he went downstairs and ate a light breakfast and then, following a gut instinct he had that the woman from the night before and Aneta's murder were somehow related, decided to go find Skylar and convince her to come with him to see the police and ferret out this lead her uncle mentioned.

Frankly, he wasn't sure what else to do. If Luca Futura was the murdering son of a bitch Cole's brothers were convinced he was, Cole had to find some way to prove it. Either that, or exact revenge. Any which way, it was obvious Skylar wouldn't want a thing to do with him before this was over.

HE DROVE TO THE GALLERY in his rental car and parked on the street. The gallery had a closed look to it although it was almost noon. Sure enough, when he got to the door he found a sign he knew translated into "not open." But there was a light coming from the back where the office was located, so he rapped his knuckles against the wooden door and waited, knocking again when his first attempt brought no response.

Eventually he could see movement coming through the gallery, but it didn't appear to be Skylar. The door opened, and he was suddenly face-to-face with a gray-haired man in his late fifties with round black glasses and a hook nose that made him look like a hungry eagle.

Doubting the guy spoke English, Cole gave it a shot anyway. "I'm looking for Skylar Pope."

The man furrowed his brow, then nodded quickly as he touched his balding head. "You mean girl with purple stripe? No, no, she leave gallery."

"When?"

The man shrugged. "I don't look at clock. Not long. Five, ten minutes? She get call and rush out."

"Did she say where she was going?"

"She say nothing. Okay, she say something about painting and then run out of here like feet on fire."

"Did she go toward the bus?"

He waved his hand down the block. "That way."

The opposite direction from the bus. "And who exactly are you, sir?" Cole asked.

"I give audit for Ms. Ables," he said, his voice impatient. "You to come back next week." And then the door closed and that was that.

Skylar had told him the night they went to dinner that she didn't drive to work because of the downtown traffic. She preferred to take the bus, but that didn't mean she didn't occasionally drive herself. However, if she had driven, wouldn't she have parked in the alley instead of the street? The fact she'd left through the front door and hurried away from the bus station seemed significant to him. Wherever she went was probably within walking distance, but that could cover a lot of possibilities.

What was going on?

He took off down the sidewalk, pausing to look through every business window, opening doors and checking inside when he couldn't see through the glass, a growing sense of urgency propelling him forward.

Chapter Seven

"Where did you get this?" Skylar asked the shop owner, a man who was almost as wide around the middle as he was tall. With his closely cropped hair and pear shape, he resembled a bowling pin.

"I assure you it's genuine. But it is not yet for sale. Another few weeks, you come back and we'll see."

Skylar looked through the case window at the Bartow miniature painting, unframed, resting on a small easel. Mr. Machnik's painting.

She was in a cluttered shop where the merchandise traveled the gamut from dusty, old and worthless to electronics to this piece of valuable art. She imagined the place was the equivalent of a pawn shop back home. If so, Aneta had brought the painting here, taken a percentage of its worth in the informal terms of a loan and intended to buy it back, including interest, when the month was over.

Only Aneta would never come back.

How had she thought she could ever get away with that?

Answer? She hadn't. She hadn't planned to return for the painting, probably hadn't planned to return to Traterg, period. She'd just needed cash....

And it had apparently gotten her killed.

"This is stolen property," Skylar said. "You have to call the police."

"No, it is not stolen."

Skylar started to ask him what "the girl" had looked like when she caught sight of a rolled-up copy of the newspaper up on his desk behind the counter. "May I see that paper?" she asked, gesturing at the desk.

He turned laboriously, scooped up the paper in a fleshy hand and handed it to Skylar, who unrolled and divided it into sections. What she was looking for was the cover story for the Metro section, and she turned the paper so the shop owner could see the accompanying photograph of Aneta Cazo taken the year before with her much younger sister.

"Is that the girl who brought the painting into your shop?" Skylar asked.

He started to shake his head and then picked up the paper and peered at it, his expressionless eyes narrowing, nostrils flaring.

"She was murdered two days ago," Skylar added.

He licked his lips. "Murdered?"

"Yes. She stole that painting from my aunt's gallery. It belongs to one of our customers. Aneta brought it to you, and you gave her money."

"But she said the painting had been her dead grandmother's possession and that it had passed to her."

"Did she provide a providence for the painting?"

"Well, no."

"Don't you have to report your dealings to the police at the end of each day?"

His gaze shifted, and she got the distinct feeling that he'd skirted that detail of the law—at least this one time. "Did she say why she needed money?"

He met her gaze again, on firmer ground now. "To help her sister. She had to travel."

"Where?"

"Why would she tell me that?"

Good point. "Was she nervous? Upset?"

There was a bell at the door signaling a newcomer, but neither Skylar nor the shopkeeper looked up. He shrugged. "Lots of people are nervous when they come here. This is a legitimate business, but people sometimes regard it as unsavory."

"Hmm…well, the painting must be put in a safe until the police can get here," Skylar said. "I'm calling them right now."

She took out her cell, but before she could place the call, someone touched her shoulder. Startled, she turned right into Cole.

Grasping her chest with one hand, she said, "Geez, you snuck up on me," switching to English effortlessly.

"Blame years of stealth training," he said with a warm smile that spread an equally cozy glow through her body.

"I have to call Detective Kilo," she said and placed the call. Kilo was unavailable, she was told, but they would send someone immediately.

"I tried calling you from the hotel," he said.

"I've been running around," she explained, leaving out the part about how she'd recognized the hotel phone number and decided not to answer his call. The night before still made her want to blush. She wasn't ready to talk to him. However, that was now a moot point as he was standing here, in the flesh, as big and sexy and real as a man could possibly get. She pointed at the painting under the counter. "That's the Bartow that went missing."

"I figured," he said, gazing at it. "Tiny little thing, isn't it?"

"Yes. But look at the colors."

"Are you sure that's it?"

"Positive. I spent two hours fitting it with a frame, remember? I know every brushstroke. Besides, this shopkeeper identified Aneta from her photograph in the newspaper."

He stood very close as he studied the painting. The shopkeeper stood off at his desk, arms folded across his curiously narrow chest, gaze averted. It was obvious he wasn't going to move the painting until the police demanded he do so. It didn't really matter as Skylar planned on standing there until they arrived. No way would she let Mr. Machnik's painting get away from her twice.

What was far more disconcerting was the heat radiating from Cole. It was like he had a switch that he could turn on when he wanted to make her feel faint. But that same switch could also turn to off, giving her the unshakable impression that a war waged inside his soldier-trained body that in some indefinable way included her.

They waited around until the police showed up, and Skylar verified the painting was the one Aneta had taken from its frame. She had hoped Detective Kilo himself would come, but it was just a bored-looking guy in a uniform. When they were free to leave, she and Cole walked along the sidewalk side by side.

"How's your head?" she asked.

As she expected he would, he passed off her concern. "It's fine. How in the world did you find that painting?"

"By luck. One of our loyal customers haunts places like that one. She'd read about the theft and Aneta's death, and when she saw the unframed Bartow, she called the gallery and told me about it. I rushed right over there." She told him Aneta's cover story, that she'd inherited the painting and needed some quick cash to go on a trip to help her sister.

"Do you think there's any truth in it?" he asked. "I don't mean about the painting per se but the sister part?"

"She does have a sister although I never heard Aneta talk about her. The girl looks to be in her early teens. I've only seen her photo in the paper. The article said her family lives in a little town northeast of here on the road to Slovo."

"Are you familiar with Slovo?"

"I've been there. Just in the summer. My aunt used to take me when I visited as a kid. There's an old castle on an island in the middle of a lake that's been turned into a hotel. Very charming."

He nodded, and once again, he managed to look as though he was struggling to keep things to himself. "So how did you know where to find me?" she added after several seconds of silent walking.

"The man doing your aunt's audit described you getting the call and running off in this direction."

"I'm surprised he noticed. When that guy gets going with his numbers, the rest of the world tends to fade away."

Cole stopped and, gently grasping her shoulders, he turned her to face him. "Maybe the man has a thing for captivating women with colorful stripes in their hair."

She smiled as she shook her head. "Somehow, I doubt it."

"Listen," Cole added, pulling her closer to the building to let pedestrians pass. "About last night—"

"Oh, please, let's not have this conversation right now. Please." She looked away, awkward and uneasy. She'd had hours to think about his switch from steaming hot to icy-cold and still didn't know what to make of it except that she would never allow herself to be that vulnerable with a near-stranger again. The only thing she was positive about was that it wasn't his bashed head or her kissing ability that had made him pull away. So what had happened?

"If that's the way you want it," he said.

"That's the way I want it. I made a mistake."

"If there was a mistake, then it was mine."

"This is coming perilously close to talking about it," she warned, holding up a hand.

"All right. So, new subject. Did your uncle say anything more about the lead he mentioned last night?"

She narrowed her eyes as she regarded him.

"What is it?" he asked.

She shook her head. She was thinking about her uncle's observation that Cole happened to be at the gallery when she needed help with the painting and the suggestion that perhaps that hadn't been an accident. Cole sure seemed interested in everything to do with Aneta.

Could he be involved in her death somehow? Is that why her killer hadn't turned around and shot him on the fire escape? Was it possible his showing up at the gallery and every time since then had less to do with chance and her quirky charms than his own agenda?

"Do you have to go back to the gallery?" he asked.

Coming on the heels of their recent conversation, no way was she going to admit that for a few days, at least, she was as good as out of a job. He might suggest going back to the hotel or eating a quiet, intimate meal. She could tell herself she would not fall victim to his charms again, but she had to face it that it was banking on willpower she seemed to lose the minute he touched her.

"I have errands to run," she said at last.

"Would you consider accompanying me to the police station so we can ask Detective Kilo about this so-called lead?" Cole asked.

That should be safe. "Okay." It might be interesting seeing him interact with the police.

The trouble was that Cole confused her. She was attracted to his looks, to his strength, even to the secrets she knew coursed through his veins as surely as did his own blood. He was more than he appeared, and the safe, rational thing to do would be to ask him to leave her alone and stick to it.

He took her hand and looked down at her palm as though weighing something important. And then he laced his fingers through hers and squeezed. Her heart skipped a few beats.

Okay, so she wasn't going to tell him to go away—not quite yet, anyway.

COLE KNEW SKYLAR WAS his ticket to an audience with Kilo, and talking to Kilo was the only thing he could think to do between now and leaving for Slovo in the morning.

Experience said several unusual things happening at once within the same perimeter were likely to be connected. So in some strange way, he was pretty sure Aneta's apparently uncustomary foray into thievery, her subsequent murder, the half-belligerent middle-aged woman fixated on Ian Banderas *and* the way it all circled around the life of Luca Futura had to be somehow related.

But how?

And even if he uncovered the how, would it lead him to the irrefutable proof he needed to exact revenge? Or was it just an unimportant diversion?

Revenge. The word brought up terrible images in Cole's mind—images of wars and suffering where one side does something terrible to the other side and they retaliate, and so on and so on. Each exchange ups the stakes, becomes more and more intense, the acts of aggression increasingly hostile and violent.

And there were always innocent casualties along the way; in this case, that would be Skylar's aunt and Skylar herself. When the time came, would Cole have the stomach to hurt them under the banner of justice, trying to exact revenge on a deed committed three decades before?

He remembered Skylar mentioning her uncle's policy of not allowing coworkers, especially underlings, to get too familiar. He'd reportedly said he had firsthand experience how that could backfire.

Was that experience gained when he did that very thing to his own boss? Had he learned the lesson by living it in reverse? And then there was that tune, the same one his brother Tyler admitted he'd been whistling and humming since he was a little kid, buried so deep in his subconscious now that it was a habit, a memory whose origin was vague at best.

"What did your uncle do after the ambassador was killed?" he asked Skylar as they approached the police station.

She cast him what he was beginning to think of as her suspicious look. Not that he didn't deserve it. "I'm not sure," she said. "That was before I was born, years before I even started coming here. My uncle doesn't talk about it much. Why do you ask?"

He tried a nonchalant shrug. "Curiosity. He's a very impressive man."

"Yes, he is. He's been a wonderful husband for my aunt and a good uncle to me and my brothers and sisters," Skylar said, her gaze darting up to meet his. "That's what Uncle Luca is to me—family."

They entered the station and were ultimately shown into Detective Kilo's office. The place smelled like an ashtray, and Kilo's yellow-toothed smile of welcoming seemed a little forced.

"Sit down, Ms. Pope, Mr. Bennett," he said. "I only have a moment or two before a meeting."

Cole spoke up. "Mr. Futura mentioned a lead in Aneta Cazo's murder."

Kilo leaned back in his chair, crossed his hands on his stomach and stared at Cole. "May I ask why you are inquiring about this lead?"

Skylar sat forward. "Aneta was my coworker and my aunt's employee. Before she died, she stole a painting from my aunt's vault and hocked it as I'm sure you've been informed. We found her body. I found the painting. Why wouldn't we be interested in how the investigation is going? Besides, if my uncle was going to discuss it with us before a business matter diverted his attention, I'm not sure why you're so reticent."

Kilo snapped back upright, snatched a stack of papers from his desktop and made a big deal out of stacking them, squaring them by tapping them on his desk. Carefully setting them aside, he finally spoke. "I am a policeman, Ms. Pope. Cautious is just part of who I am. As for the lead your uncle was going to mention, it is ongoing and concerns an…acquaintance of Ms. Cazo's."

"An acquaintance? You mean a boyfriend?"

"Exactly."

"What about the painting and her telling the shopkeeper she needed to travel to help her sister?"

"The woman was a liar. Her murder was undoubtedly a miserable end to a squalid love affair. I am no longer on the case."

"Then who is?"

"I don't know. I was told to direct my attention to a string of attacks on tourists. We can't have that."

Cole and Skylar both sat back, a little too surprised to react.

"And so, if you will excuse me."

"How do we find out who is in charge of the case now?" Skylar finally said. "My aunt and uncle—"

"Your uncle is aware of everything that happens here, Ms. Pope."

"But he would—"

"You are an American," he added. "Maybe things are run differently in your country. But here we neither encourage nor desire the public to take part in our investigations." He stood abruptly and added, "And now, if you will excuse me, I am late for that appointment I mentioned."

And don't let the door hit you on your way out, his tone added.

"So, what's going on?" Cole asked as they left the building.

"I don't have the slightest idea."

"Kilo was different than before. Less solicitous of you, for one thing, as though he was angry about something."

She nodded. She'd noticed that, too.

He stopped her at the bottom of the steps. "I have to go to Slovo tomorrow to meet with a distributor," he said. "If you come with me, we could stop and see if we can find the town Aneta's family comes from. Maybe they would have answers."

"Answers to what, exactly?" she said.

"To what was bothering Aneta. Was she having an affair? Had she talked to them about leaving? Stuff like that. And then after I meet with my distributor, you could give me the grand tour of Slovo by night."

"That's a five-minute adventure," she said.

"But we'd have the whole day together," he said, leaning close enough to kiss her.

"It sounds like fun, but I think I'll have to pass," she said.

"You know how to reach me if you change your mind," he said.

"Yes, I do."

They walked in silence toward the gallery. "Will you have dinner with me tonight?" he asked as they approached his rental car.

"I can't," she said.

He met her gaze and held it. "Or won't?"

She tilted her head. "I guess a little of both. My uncle left a note this morning asking me to be home this evening for my aunt. I can't leave. She's very upset about Aneta. It's like the more she thinks about it, the worse she feels."

What Skylar didn't add was her determination to talk to her uncle about Ian Banderas and the odd and dangerous woman stalking him. She didn't want to get Cole any more involved than he already was.

"That's the *can't* part," he said. "What's the *won't* part?" When she didn't immediately respond, he added, "This has to do with last night, doesn't it?"

"We're going way too fast," she said. "And it's not just your fault. When it comes to you, I lack a certain amount of self-control. But there's more. You're not being entirely frank with me, and that makes me nervous."

He opened his mouth as if to protest, then seemed to think better of it. "Doesn't everybody have secrets?"

"Probably. Secrets between friends is one thing. But between lovers, it's another. Too risky."

"So, I'm too dangerous to justify the risk?" he whispered, leaning closer.

Take a breath. "Yes."

"I may be worth it," he whispered as his lips landed on hers, warm, soft and full of what the hell, life is short. Despite everything, she had to admit she welcomed his kiss, at least for a moment, then she pulled away. "That doesn't help."

"When it comes to this particular matter, my goal isn't to be helpful." He kissed her forehead and her cheek. "I want to finish what we started last night," he whispered. His words ricocheted through her body.

"Now that your head is all better," she added.

"Exactly."

She pulled away and looked him in the eye. "You're lying to me."

He stared at her, his blue eyes unfathomable, and as usual, the feeling there was something bubbling right under the surface was impossible to ignore. "Listen, Cole, if you ever decide to come clean with me, let me know, okay?"

"Is there no way you can trust I would never hurt you?" he said with a gaze that devoured her.

"I hate to rattle off a cliché, but trust has to be earned."

"And I haven't earned it?"

"Can you honestly say you aren't hiding something important from me?"

His gaze delved so deep it reached all the way to her heart and beyond. She was afraid to breathe. All he had to do was tell her she was letting her imagination get away with her. It's what she wanted to hear.

"No, I can't," he said. "I'm sorry."

Chapter Eight

"How well did you really know Aneta?" Skylar asked her aunt. They had settled in her aunt's suite after a light supper. Eleanor Ables lay on the lounge, bundled in blankets trying to stay warm in a room already too hot.

Skylar waited for an answer while sewing a row of tiny red buttons onto her newest creation, a short woolen skirt with a flattering flare. She'd finished the matching jacket a week before, and it kind of startled her to realize that was before she'd met Cole, before Aneta's murder, before everything changed.

Her aunt finally responded. "I've been trying to think. Two years, maybe a little longer. She answered an ad I placed in the newspaper. You should have seen her. Pretty, of course, but very poor and it showed. I took her to my salon, got her a good haircut and gave her some clothes that didn't fit me anymore. She changed from a little weed to a lovely flower."

"Were you close to her?"

"In a way," her aunt said, dabbing at her eyes with a tissue. "Aneta had a kind of natural reserve. She wasn't the type of girl who gushed about boyfriends or movies."

"Did she talk about her sister?"

"Occasionally. Once she asked if it was okay if she gave her sister a sweater I had given her. I told her of

course it was okay. It was hers to do with as she pleased."
More wiping of the eyes and she looked at Skylar with a
haunted expression. "You know I couldn't have children.
Aneta filled that void a little in her way. I can't believe
she would steal something from me."

"I guess, technically, she didn't," Skylar said. "Many
of your things were much more valuable than Mr. Machnik's painting, but that's what she took."

Skylar's aunt actually looked cheered by this take on
the facts. "I want to know what happened to her no matter how awful it is. Luca won't tell me anything that he
believes will upset me, so I'll have to depend on you.
Promise me that you'll let me know the truth."

"Of course," Skylar said.

"Good. Luca can be so protective."

Skylar snipped the thread and stuck the needle in the
pincushion as there was a light rapping on her aunt's
door. A moment later, Skylar's uncle entered the room.
He looked pretty exhausted as he crossed the floor to kiss
his wife and pat Skylar's head.

"Eleanor, dearest, it's late. You should be asleep," he
said, casting a scowl at the nurse.

"Don't blame Greta," Eleanor said, referring to her
caretaker. "Skylar and I have been visiting." She cast Skylar a look that clearly warned not to confide in Luca what
she had asked Skylar to do. "But I am tired," she added.

Skylar stood up and stretched, kind of glad to get a reprieve from the sweltering bedroom yet dreading the long,
sleepless night ahead of her. She knew as soon as her brain
stopped sweating that she'd start thinking about Cole.

"May I talk to you for a few minutes when you're done
in here?" she asked her uncle, her voice soft so as not to
alarm her aunt.

"Of course. Wait for me in my study?"

"Okay. Shall I have the cook send you up a late supper?"

"Thank you, no. I ate hours ago," he said. "I'll be along in a minute."

As she closed the door behind her, she heard her uncle humming the lullaby and glanced back over her shoulder. He sat on the bed beside Aunt Eleanor, holding her hand, his eyes closed.

Skylar deposited her sewing supplies in her room and hung the skirt in the closet, then went along to her uncle's study. She was a little nervous about burdening him with any more problems, but she had the feeling he was used to getting to the bottom of things and she didn't need to protect him. The more she thought about it, the more she agreed with Cole: Banderas was up to no good, and if that was true, then she owed it to her uncle to alert him to it.

Thinking of Cole made a well of despair open in her gut. She'd as good as kissed him off today, and for the life of her, she couldn't pinpoint one solid reason for doing so. They'd only known each other for a handful of days; what made her think she had the right to know all his secrets? Wasn't that just a little bit presumptuous? And couldn't she have just refused to sleep with him until they got to know each other better? Isn't that what normal people do?

Uncle Luca arrived as she was sitting down in front of his big ornate desk, a gift from her aunt on their twentieth wedding anniversary. It was hard to look at that highly carved antique and not wonder who else had sat behind it. Old furniture and old houses always seem to carry ghosts along with them.

"Would you like a brandy?" he asked, pausing at the built-in bar.

"That would be nice," she said, mainly to be sociable.

He handed her a small snifter. The heady fumes of the

brandy assailed her nose as she swirled the glass. He sat down, his arms resting on the desktop, his hands folded around his glass. "You look troubled," he said. "Is there anything I can do?"

She took a deep breath, unsure where to start. How did you tell a man he might have trouble in his own office? "You might have trouble in your office," she blurted out.

His eyebrows inched up his forehead. "What?"

"Ian Banderas."

His expression froze. "What about him?"

She set the untouched snifter aside and got to her feet. "There's a woman obsessed with him in some way."

"Well, I suppose he's not a bad-looking fellow."

"No, not like that. She's twenty years older than him. I've seen her twice now. The first time she was pleading with him. I don't know what she wanted, but she was so distraught you could feel it in the air. The second time she apparently followed him to this house. She hit Cole Bennett by mistake, thinking it was Ian."

"Who is this woman?"

"Her name is Svetlana Dacho. She seems to be convinced Ian is responsible for her daughter's disappearance."

Her uncle took a sip of his brandy, frowning into the glass. "The name means nothing to me," he said at last. "You say she hit Cole Bennett?"

"Yes, right outside your house. It was very dark, and she mistook him for Ian."

"Are you sure?"

"What?"

"Are you sure she wasn't really waiting to attack Mr. Bennett?"

For a moment, Skylar sat there, her mind racing

through the events of the night before. "I'm certain," she said at last. "Positive."

"Well, I'm not," he said.

"Uncle Luca, please, trust me on this. She was horrified when she saw who she'd clobbered. She kept saying she killed the wrong man. And when Ian Banderas's name was mentioned, she ran off into the dark."

"I will talk with him, of course," her uncle said. "No doubt this woman is the mother of some girlfriend of Ian's who she felt Ian led astray. I can assure you she is wrong."

Was her uncle so determined to give Ian Banderas a fair deal that he wasn't really hearing what Skylar had to say? She was frustrated at her inability to communicate her concern and worried, too, that her uncle's lack of response on this matter could come back to haunt him if Ian was as shady as Skylar was beginning to think he was.

"I also spoke to Detective Kilo today," she said. "He's been taken off Aneta's murder case."

"Did you search him out?" he asked.

"Yes. I wanted to know about the lead you mentioned."

"You went alone?"

"No. After I found the stolen painting—do you know about that?"

"Yes. Kilo informed me it had been recovered and would be returned to Mr. Machnik as soon as possible. You were saying?"

"I met up with Cole, and we decided to talk to Kilo together."

A knot formed in her uncle's jaw. He tossed down the rest of his brandy and got to his feet, coming to stand near Skylar where she'd paused her pacing to stand next to the bookcase that was covered with decades of family photos.

"This man is everywhere," he said.

"You mean Cole?" she asked, looking up from the image of her twelve-year-old self fishing on Lake Slovo.

"Yes. I think it wise if you curtail seeing him again."

"Because?"

"Because I get the distinct impression he's a trouble-maker. I do not want him in this house again."

"That's your decision, of course," she said. "However, whether I see him outside your house is mine."

He smiled. "You think I'm treating you like a child?"

"A little bit," she said with a small laugh.

"Forgive me. It's an occupational hazard of a fond uncle. Basically, you are a stranger here. This is the first time you've lived and worked in Kanistan for more than a week or two at a time. Your aunt would never forgive me if something happened to you. How can I not try to protect you?"

She smiled up at him. "I promise I'll use my head, okay?"

He gave her a quick hug. "If only that were enough."

"When did Kilo tell you that I found the painting?"

"I'm not sure," he said. "Does it matter?"

"I'm just wondering who took him off Aneta's murder investigation. I mean, was it before or after the painting was recovered? Whichever, he seemed perturbed by it."

"Maybe he had other matters on his mind," her uncle offered. "Of course, I know little about how the police work, but I am sure the job is extremely stressful."

There he went again, protecting her. Kilo had said her uncle knew everything that went on in the police office, and her uncle was telling her he didn't know how it was run. The truth probably lay somewhere in the middle.

"I beg you not to concern yourself with these tawdry matters," he said as he moved back toward his desk. "Is there anything else I can do for you? It's growing late, and I have a few calls to make yet tonight."

"No. Good night, Uncle Luca."

"Good night, my dear," he said. "And, Skylar, just be warned that I will look after you any way I must. To do less would be negligent."

She started to protest again, but what was the use? He was a proud and stubborn man, and as long as she was a guest in his house, he would demand she play by his rules. Perhaps not out-and-out verbally, but the pressure was there. He was warning her that she wouldn't see Cole again as long as she was in Kanistan.

That was okay, right? Hadn't she as much as told Cole the same thing a few hours earlier? So why did it annoy her now? Her uncle was picking up the phone as she left the office, and she heard the first few words he spoke as she closed the door. "Send someone to my place—"

Someone to his place. Within a half-dozen steps, the impact of those words hit her. She'd bet money he was arranging for someone to come keep an eye on her.

She hurried to her room and threw a few things in a large carryall, then took the time to write a note that she subsequently sealed in an envelope addressed to her aunt. She propped it on her untouched pillow, then went down the servant's stairs, exiting into the kitchen that was blissfully empty.

But all that had taken time, and her uncle's office was very close by.

She let herself out the door without turning on any lights and stood in the deepest shadows for a few moments, allowing her vision to adapt to the darkness. Then, keeping to the edge of the driveway, she approached the gatehouse, well aware of the security cameras and that she was probably being watched.

The truth was she felt melodramatic and yet nervous. She did not want to alarm her uncle or her aunt, but she wasn't content to sit in her room, either, not with her aunt's pleas still ringing in her ears. She'd lived alone for several years back home, and this feeling that she was being watched—even if it was done out of concern for her—was getting old. When she got to the street, she kept walking, using the internet access on her phone to look up Svetlana Dacho's address.

It was too late for a social call, but as this visit could hardly be labeled social, she hailed a cab and felt tucked away from curious eyes as she scooted into the warm interior. She told the driver to take a circuitous route, just in case, to the general area of the city in which Svetlana lived.

At least the late hour would probably guarantee she would be home. Skylar told the driver to let her out a couple of blocks further on, exited the cab and paid him, waiting until his taillights disappeared before turning around and hurrying back to the right address.

Svetlana had a mailbox in the lobby like Aneta had had, and Skylar couldn't help wishing Cole was there to climb those dark stairs with her. She sidled past a group of teenagers who whistled after her, past a couple making out on a landing, erupting at last on the fourth floor. She hurried down the hall, the feeling of oppression that had started in the hallway outside her uncle's den still with her.

She knocked rapidly. The whole thing was eerily reminiscent of knocking on Aneta's door and she shivered. But this time, it was answered almost immediately by the woman Skylar had last seen in her uncle's driveway. Though she appeared worn out and exhausted, it was the first time Skylar had seen her when she wasn't a complete emotional wreck, and she appeared a generation younger, surely not much over forty.

It was obvious from Svetlana's expression that she recognized Skylar, as well, and she immediately clutched her throat and backed away.

Skylar stepped into Svetlana's apartment and closed the door after her. "I'm not here to harm you," she said softly. "I just want some information."

"You are the niece of Luca Futura," Svetlana said.

"Yes, I am."

"He is a bad man."

"Why do you say that?" Skylar asked.

"Because he employs Ian Banderas," she said.

"May we sit down for a moment?" Skylar asked.

Svetlana cleared a chair of what appeared to be clean clothes in the process of being folded after washing. As spartan as Aneta's apartment had been, this one was cluttered, crammed with cast-off furniture and worn carpets. As Skylar sat, Svetlana perched on a corner of a sofa, twisting her hands in her lap.

"First of all, my uncle isn't a bad man. He is kind and loving to his family and very concerned about the people whose lives he touches." *He's also turning out to be something of a control freak,* she thought to herself. "Svetlana, have you ever heard of a woman named Aneta Cazo?"

"The name is familiar," Svetlana said.

Skylar sat foreword. "Really? In what context?"

Svetlana frowned in concentration. "I read it. In the newspaper. She's the woman who was murdered in her apartment a few days ago, isn't she?"

"Yes. But had you heard of her before that?"

Svetlana shook her head. "No, I don't think so. Was she a friend to my Malina?"

"I don't know," Skylar admitted. "Listen, will you

tell me again what you believe Ian Banderas did to your daughter?"

The woman popped to her feet and grabbed a framed photograph off a shelf, pushing it into Skylar's hands. It showed a girl of about fifteen sitting in the chair Skylar currently occupied. "She's lovely."

"That was taken just a few months ago. She worked at a café. That's where she met Ian Banderas. She doesn't know I know about him, but I do. The dishwasher there is a friend, and he warned me. Banderas is way too old for my Malina, too sophisticated. The next thing I know, Malina is gone, leaving me money, promising more, telling me not to tell anyone, not to worry. Where would she get money, and why would she disappear?"

"Did you ask Banderas about your daughter?"

"Not at first. I went to his apartment right after she left. I knew Banderas was at work, so I talked to the man who stands at the door. I showed him that picture of Malina, and he said he had never seen her."

"Did you believe him?"

The tears were back, running unheeded down Svetlana's cheeks. "I do not know what or who to believe, but I do know Ian was with Malina the night she disappeared."

"How do you know that?"

"Malina's friend at the café, Katerina, told me."

"Has she heard from Malina?"

"I don't think so. She is being friendly to Banderas, waiting to see what he does. We stay in touch. She has no family, and I worry for her." Svetlana dabbed at watery eyes. "I finally pretended to bump into this Ian and ask about Malina, but he said he had never heard of her. That's a lie. That was months ago. Malina's note told me to be patient. I try, but time keeps passing. The other night I decided to corner Ian in a public place and try to scare him into telling me the truth. Not one word do I hear from my girl. But he does not scare, that one. I am sorry about hitting your friend. If Banderas knew I tried to attack him, I think he might kill me. He is evil. I am so grateful he doesn't know what I did, but what do I do now?"

Skylar sat very still. She'd told her uncle this woman's name. He would innocently mention it to Ian when they spoke. What would Ian do? "Svetlana, do you have anywhere you can go for a few nights?"

The panic was back in the woman's eyes. "I must stay here in case Malina returns."

"No, you must disappear for a while." She gestured at the cell phone on the coffee table. "She can always call you, right?"

The worried frown softened a bit. "Yes, she can call."

Skylar dug in her purse and came up with most of the euros she carried. "Take this, and get a room or pay a friend for space. Something. Leave now, tonight. Right now."

Svetlana apparently grasped the urgency in Skylar's voice and gathered a clean change of clothes from the basket on the floor, shoving them into a paper sack. She picked up her phone to call her friend, and Skylar stopped her. "Don't tell anyone where you're going. Just surprise your friend."

Svetlana nodded, eyes solemn, dropping her phone into her coat pocket, but she refused to take money from Skylar. "Money is what Malina left me, but what good is money without my girl?"

Skylar called another cab, and the two women took it to Svetlana's friend's place on the outskirts of Traterg. "You will try to find what happened?" Svetlana asked as she got out of the cab. "Maybe you could ask your uncle. But don't say my name, please."

"Yes, I promise." She was making lots of promises tonight. This was one she had no right to make as it had been broken before she even got here. But reflected in Svetlana's voice was the same longing to know what was really going on that Skylar had heard in her aunt's. "It may take a couple of days," she added. "What was the name of the café Malina worked at? I take it Katerina is still there?"

"Yes, yes, for now. It's called Pushki's," Svetlana said. She grabbed Skylar's hands and squeezed them, then hurried into her friend's house.

It was very late by now, well after two in the morning, and Skylar wasn't sure what to do. If her suspicions about her uncle's intentions were correct—that he had engaged someone to follow her—they might find the note she'd left in her room. She would bet money they would settle on Cole's hotel as her likely escape.

But that's exactly where she needed to go. She needed to talk to Aneta's family to gather more information with which to get her uncle to open his eyes to his assistant's escapades. And she needed Cole's help to do that.

But she'd told him to back off. How did she go back on that a mere twelve hours later?

The night staff was sparse at the hotel, but someone eventually noticed Skylar lurking behind the plants and came to see if there was something wrong. She made up a story about a jealous boyfriend and heaven knows what else until the poor clerk took pity on her and allowed her to rent a room for the remainder of the night without formally registering. She paid in cash and went to her room, which wasn't half as plush as Cole's room.

She sat on the bed and wondered what she was doing there. When her uncle found out she'd left the way she did, his feelings would be hurt, and that wasn't her goal. Maybe she should just go back to the house, try talking to him again, maybe borrow her aunt's car and drive to see Aneta's family by herself.

What had happened to her? Her whole life, she'd been the sunny girl who never seemed to have trouble with anything or anyone. She'd trusted everyone she knew and loved and thought she understood exactly who they were and what they wanted.

And now she felt as if she'd lost her way, that the map she'd been following had somehow been torn in half and she was missing the directions she needed to make wise decisions.

She left a wake-up call for early in the morning and doubted she would need it. Sleep seemed like something she'd done in a past life when her brain knew how to relax. Tonight, it just raced….

COLE SAT DOWN AT the counter in the hotel coffee shop as he had most mornings since arriving in Traterg. He wasn't looking forward to the three-hour-or-more drive to Slovo and was still trying to decide if he should try to look up Aneta's family. Without Skylar to bridge the language barrier, what was the point?

The waitress set a cup of strong coffee down in front of him, and he nodded at her. He pointed at the picture on the menu that illustrated a stack of toasted bread. She apparently got the drift of his meaning because she walked off to give his order to the kitchen.

The sugar was on the other side of the person sitting next to him, who was buried in a newspaper. He tapped his neighbor on the arm. The paper shifted slightly, and he found himself looking into an alpine lake, or rather two eyes the color of one.

"Skylar?"

"Shh." She was dressed simply in jeans and a bulky

sweater and wore a wool knit cap pulled down over her hair. Keeping the newspaper high, she added, "I think someone may be following me."

"Who?" he asked, although the bigger question was why.

"No idea. I don't want to go into it all right this second, but can I change my mind and go with you to Slovo?"

He was still getting over the shock of her presence. He'd written off his chances of ever seeing her again; yesterday's conversation had revealed she sensed he wasn't being forthright and he'd admired her for putting her foot down and drawing a line. Regretted it, sure, but admired it, too. Skylar Pope might look like an ingenue with her china-blue eyes and perfect skin, but she was no one's fool.

Yet here she was. "Why the change of heart?" he said knowing he should shut up and enjoy providence or whatever had caused it.

Him, maybe? Was it possible she'd regretted not coming back to the hotel with him? He knew he had missed her horribly and had spent a good part of the night waiting for a tentative knock on his door, a soft voice. Dare he hope against all reason that she felt the same way?

"Can't a woman be fickle on occasion?" she said.

He looked deep into her eyes. "Hell, yes."

"I hear a *but* in your voice," she said softly.

"But I really didn't expect to see you again."

She looked hard at him and then away. "I see."

"You see what?"

"You've found someone else."

"Now wait a second. You've got it all wrong."

She glanced back at him again. "I need to talk to Aneta's family in Chiaro. I would rather not go alone, but if you've made other plans, I can borrow my aunt's car."

He rested his hand lightly on her thigh. "I haven't made other plans. Of course, you can come."

She sighed with relief. "Thank you."

"I have to be in Slovo by four."

"Then we'd better leave pretty soon, right?"

"Yes," he said. "Have you eaten?"

"I'm not hungry."

"And you refuse to tell me what's going on?"

"I'll tell you when we get away from here." She folded the newspaper back around her face as the waitress delivered a plate of crusty toast along with a glass bowl of the tart fruit spread he'd grown to appreciate. But now his appetite was off, too, as though Skylar's anxiety had transferred itself to him. He took a cautious glance around the café, but no one was looking at him or Skylar.

"I'll go get the car," he said after a couple of bites that tasted like cardboard.

She met his gaze. "I'll walk down the block and meet you on the corner."

"Give me a few minutes. I have to go back to my room for my coat and things." Before he left, he posed another question. "Are you in danger?"

"Of course not," she said quickly, her voice evincing surprise at the question. "Who would I be in danger from?"

"I don't know. But this cloak-and-dagger stuff is a little…suggestive."

"I just want to go my own way without being followed like a troublesome child," she said.

He kept his mouth shut, but that didn't mean he hadn't noticed the slight pause before she answered and the way her gaze jumped around.

What had happened between the time she told him she was through with him and her showing up here hiding behind newspapers, begging him to help her find answers she hadn't cared about the day before?

And what had happened to his resolve to find a way to use this woman without becoming emotionally involved with her? Obviously, life had finally accomplished what he would have once thought impossible: finding a way around his best intentions.

Chapter Nine

"Can you tell if we picked up a tail?" Skylar asked, adjusting the mirrors to view the road behind them.

"I don't see anyone," he said. "When are you going to tell me what's going on?"

"Right now," she said as he merged onto the highway leading away from the city. As he drove, she told him about her conversation with her uncle, about her worry that he hadn't taken Skylar's concerns about his employee seriously enough and that his goal of protecting her from the harsh realities of his life would come back to bite him.

It was obvious to Cole that Skylar still believed in her uncle, and once again, his own doubts surfaced. He wasn't foolish enough to think that a man couldn't be cruel to one group of people and kind to another, but the disconnect between what Skylar knew of her uncle and what Cole suspected of his past were a world apart. They would never agree on this issue, and that meant there was no future for them unless he could prove he was right.

But wait, what was he thinking? This wasn't about the future. This was about the past, and the truth was that Skylar Pope was no longer of any use to him. She'd disclosed that her uncle had pegged Cole as a troublemaker.

So, get through this day and then announce he was leaving Traterg for good and go underground, investigate Futura from a different angle, let Skylar go. Just get through today. Maybe Irina would have information that would tie this whole thing up with a bow, and he could retreat in time to salvage something of worth.

"After I got it in my head that my uncle would have me trailed to make sure I was safe, I had to get out of that house," she said. "And now, frankly, I'm not sure how to go back."

So that's why she'd come to him.

"There's more, though," she added. "There's that woman who keeps showing up, Svetlana Dacho. Last night I went to see her. I thought maybe there was a connection between Aneta and her daughter, but it doesn't appear there is and yet she mentioned a friend of her daughter's, a girl named Katerina who also works at the café and who is apparently spending time with Banderas. Svetlana is terrified that he'll come after her if he hears she tried to kill him. Unfortunately, I told my uncle about her, including her name. He'll have no reason not to share it with Ian, so I think I've put her in danger."

"And what does all this have to do with Aneta?"

"Uncovering why Aneta stole that painting is important to my aunt, who also wants to know why Aneta was murdered and is afraid my uncle will keep the truth from her in an effort to protect her. It's clear to me the police don't really care one way or another who killed Aneta."

"I agree," he said. Now he knew why Skylar had changed her mind about coming—not because of him, because of her aunt. In a way, it was a relief. But, truthfully, it was also a disappointment.

"I'm sorry about yesterday," she said as though tuned into his thoughts. "I got cold feet and came off very righteous. I don't know what got into me."

He shook his head. "Don't apologize for looking out for yourself," he said.

"You say that with such feeling."

"You have good instincts. That's all I'm saying."

They drove in silence for a while as the traffic thinned and the countryside became more rural. He'd looked at a map the night before and knew Chiaro was a very small town off the main highway, tucked into the mountains. He hoped the roads weren't icy or blocked. It would take at least two hours to drive from there to Slovo, somehow unload Skylar and go meet with Irina. Better make it three to be safe. That left them just a couple of hours in Chiaro.

THE TOWN WAS SMALL, GRITTY, industrial and located in a pass where the major business seemed to be the enormous train switching yard on the outskirts through which they entered. The skies were overcast anyway, so the weak light coupled with the clanging of train cars and sooty atmosphere made it feel like they'd left one country and entered another.

"Slow down," Skylar said. "I looked up the Cazo family on the internet last night in my hotel room. There are a lot of them here in Chiaro, but I'm almost positive Aneta mentioned the name Inna once. There's an Inna Cazo on a street that translates to Depot Way."

"As in *train depot?*"

"I don't know for sure, but it sounds reasonable."

It took forty minutes of driving and backtracking before they finally found the right house, a two-story dark gray brick building that kind of squatted on a patch of earth dusted with snow.

They approached it warily. If this was the right house, the family might well be suspicious about people claiming to know their daughter who was murdered a mere four days before.

There was no bell to ring, so Cole knocked firmly, glancing down at Skylar and trying out an encouraging smile. As usual, just the sight of her face warmed him in continually unexpected ways.

After a moment or two, the door was opened by a woman who appeared to be in her seventies dressed head to toe in black.

Skylar started speaking at once, her voice soft and respectful and yet rapid as though she was afraid the woman would tell her to get lost. The one word he caught was the name: *Inna.* The woman nodded, her lips parting to reveal a smile minus a tooth or two. She seemed a little old to be Aneta's mother, and hadn't Skylar told him Aneta had a younger sister, as well? How was this possible? Maybe poverty and hard work had aged the woman far beyond her years.

The woman broke into a tearful smile and opened her arms. Skylar embraced her, wiping tears from her own cheeks as she answered what sounded like a slew of questions. Then she tugged Cole's hand, and they stepped inside. The house smelled like roasting vegetables.

After settling them on a sofa cluttered with doilies, the older woman disappeared up the steep stairs, climbing slowly as though her hips hurt.

"Is that Aneta's mother?" he whispered to Skylar.

"No, that's her grandmother. It's *her* name Aneta mentioned, not her mother's. Burian is Aneta's father. He works at the train yard. Anyway, Inna is going upstairs to see if Aneta's mother, Yelena, will speak with us. I gather she's getting ready for work. Things have been tough around here lately."

"Yeah," he said. The house had a chill that went deeper than the snow outside or the paucity of coal on the grate.

The old woman reappeared—alone. She and Skylar talked for several minutes, their voices soft and their speech quick. A noise on the stairwell caught Cole's attention, and he looked up to find a woman of about forty with dark hair and way too much makeup hurling herself down the stairs. She looked from Cole to Skylar. "You are Aneta's friends?" she cried in passable English.

The old woman said something to her, but the younger woman, who had to be Yelena, shook her head, responded in kind and then zeroed in on Skylar. "There's not much time," she said, glancing at her watch.

"I worked with her, yes," Skylar said in English. "Inna told me your younger daughter is missing?"

Yelena spared a dismissive look at her mother. "Not missing. She had a great opportunity in America, and she took it."

"How old is she?"

"Zina is fourteen. Why? Do you have news about who killed Aneta?"

"No, I'm afraid I don't," Skylar said. Aneta's mother's face crumbled just as her own mother's had, but her eyes stayed dry. Given the heavy mascara that went with the red lips and rouged cheeks, that was probably just as well.

"You must leave," she said. "It's almost noon. I must be at work soon and Burian—he comes home for lunch."

"Please," Skylar persisted. "Did you know that Aneta stole a valuable piece of art right before she died and that she said she needed money to travel to help her sister?"

"My Aneta did not steal," Yelena said. "I do not believe this story."

"It's true," Skylar said. "Where was she going to go to help her sister? Do you know?"

"I tell you it is all lies! Who would she steal from? That rich American woman who is married to Luca Futura?

Who would steal from such a woman with a husband like that? You are saying bad things about Aneta because she is not here to defend herself."

"But what about Zina?"

The back door slammed. Both the older women immediately glanced at each other and then away as a man entered the room from what must be the kitchen. He was a big guy, easily as tall as Cole and fifty pounds heavier, wearing dark jeans and a heavy jacket that increased his bulk. His face was set in a terrible scowl, and he yelled at Aneta's grandmother, who tried to placate him. She used the name *Burian* in response. So this was Aneta's father.

With his arrival, the already semi-hostile atmosphere instantly deteriorated. The man stood with hands clenched at his sides, ignoring Skylar, casting Cole a steady, menacing glare.

Great. All Cole needed was a fight with a grieving, angry man. He raised his hands open-palmed in front of him, hoping the guy understood the universal sign for "Hey, Dude, no problems." Burian growled a few sentences to his wife and laughed, which was fine with Cole. The grandmother spoke, and Burian advanced on her as though he meant to backhand her into silence. Cole's muscles tightened. He might not fight for himself right this minute, but he'd be damned if he would stand there and watch the man hit an old woman.

Yelena caught Burian's arm and held him back. She said something to him, and he waved her off, scowling at Cole before returning to the kitchen. Aneta's grandmother hovered near the door, neither in the room nor outside it.

"He is just home for a while. You must leave," Yelena said.

"I don't understand your lack of concern for Zina," Skylar persisted.

"I told you," Yelena whispered. "Zina went to America. She left me money she knew I needed."

"Where did she get the money?"

She lowered her voice. "From a wealthy woman who admired Zina's excellent work."

"Her work?"

"At the café where I am hostess. No one knows Zina is my daughter. There is a policy about families working together. Anyway, this woman offered Zina a big opportunity and she took it, so do not worry about her. And don't tell Burian about the money. He would drink it away if given the chance. Go, now."

"I think you should be worried about Zina," Skylar said as Inna shooed them toward the door. "There's another girl about the same age who also disappeared under very similar circumstances."

"Zina rode on a jet all the way to America, and someday I will join her and maybe even Grandma, too. Just not Burian. He has the terrible temper. She is fine, that one. She is strong. It is Aneta who is dead."

"Have you ever heard of a man named Ian Banderas?"

"No. I do not know that name," Yelena said. "Now, please, you must go."

"America?" Cole said. "Why would some woman offer to pay a kid's way to America?"

"I should have asked her what the woman looked like," Skylar said, checking the visor mirror, more out of habit than because she expected she would find someone back there trailing them. "It was tense, wasn't it? Especially at the last?"

"Yeah."

"It's obvious both women are scared to death of Burian. That's what Yelena was telling me before Inna came downstairs. Inna didn't come down at first because she was afraid to talk to us with her husband due to arrive soon. I guess the thought we might have news about Aneta's murder changed her mind."

"Where does the mother work? That was some pretty heavy-duty makeup."

"As a hostess somewhere. She was late for work because she'd been crying all morning. Maybe that's why she slapped on the makeup a little heavy. Anyway, according to Inna, Aneta did not have a new boyfriend, so her excuse for her distraction at work doesn't seem to hold water."

"Nor does the police point of view. But I don't know—do modern young women living away from home tell their grandmothers about their boyfriends?"

"Good point," Skylar admitted. "Still, you can't get around the fact that there are lots of similarities in the way Aneta's little sister and Svetlana's daughter left home."

"Dead of night, a little note to stay quiet, a little money to pay for their patience, at least for a while. And then nothing."

"Exactly. Svetlana said her daughter was as good as dead. It gives me the chills. When we get back to Traterg, I'm going to ask Malina's girlfriend at the café where she works if Malina ever mentioned America."

"Good idea."

She took a deep breath and glanced over at him as he drove. It was strange the way he seemed so familiar and yet not. She wanted to ask him about the clown figurine she'd found in his drawer; it seemed so out of character for a guy like him to travel with something like that on a business trip, but she couldn't bring herself to invade his privacy.

What was it about him that had her coming and going?

It wasn't just his appearance or the way he looked at her or reached for her hand. It was more than that, yet on some primal level, it was all just that.

"Are you hungry?" she asked.

"I am. But this road doesn't seem to be cluttered with restaurants."

"I remembered that from the last time I traveled it. That's why I asked the kitchen to pack a picnic for two, strictly things easy to eat while driving."

"Bring it on," he said, smiling at her.

Maybe it was his smile. Sure didn't hurt. She reached for her carry-on and took out the box the kitchen had delivered at her request that morning. There were crisp crackers and pâté, bottles of sparkling water, pickles and olives, spreadable cheese. She laid it all out as well as she could on her lap and the console between the seats, and they ate while talking about the deteriorating weather as the altitude gradually climbed and the air outside grew colder. The rain that had started while they were inside Aneta's family home in Chiaro began to leave icy trails down the windows.

"Who are you going to meet with today?" she asked as she handed him a chocolate mint as dessert.

"A woman who runs a small cooperative of local women who make handcrafted items."

"Really?" She turned in the seat to smile at him. "Like with fabric, maybe? Fashion of sorts?"

"I doubt it," he said quickly.

"Then what?"

"I'm not exactly sure. My partner set it up before I bought in to the business. I guess I'll find out."

"Do you want a translator for the meeting?"

"Uh, no. She wanted us to meet alone."

"That's all right," Skylar said. "Well, Slovo isn't exactly a huge place, but there is a little museum I read about that's located at the Winter Palace Hotel that I would like to see."

"That sounds nice."

"It is. It's a castle turned into a hotel. I told you about it the other day. I've never stayed there. Anyway, I think if we're early enough, I'll have you drive me over. If you don't have time, I'll catch a cab. Then if your meeting runs late, I can eat dinner there. Is that all right?"

"Sounds good," he said.

"Just look for the bridge as we enter town," she added, gazing out the window. It had begun to snow and the world was slowly turning white. The pitter-patter of rain was gone now, and it was very quiet inside the luxury automobile.

"Do you miss your old life?" she asked.

"The army? Sometimes," he said. "But that kind of soldiering is hard on a body and soul, and eventually, most men outgrow the need for it."

"You had a *need?*" she asked, stressing the last word. "I don't understand. How can you have a need to be shot at?"

"It's not just getting shot at," he said, smiling at her as though she'd said something amusing. "It's the need to do something important that involves risking your body. Putting everything on the line, giving everything you have."

"I don't get it," she said.

"Sure you do. Why do you design clothes?"

"It's hardly the same thing."

"No, think. Why do you design clothes that you yourself might never wear?"

"Because I have to," she said.

"Exactly. Your aunt has to blow glass and your uncle has to be involved in politics and strategy. I had to be a soldier. I had a feckless youth with parents who didn't much care for me. That can make a person feel a little disorientated and worthless."

"How could anyone not care for you?" she said.

He seemed to wince at the tenderness that had snuck into her voice and she touched his leg. The gesture was meant to diffuse the impact of her words, but when he covered her hand before she could move it, the effect was exactly the opposite.

"Your parents must have been worried sick when you came home injured."

"My mother was ill. By the time I was out of the hospital and could go home to see them, she was in her grave and my father was ready to move on with his life."

"What does that mean? No, wait. They never came to see you in the hospital?"

"Mom was too sick to travel, so I understood how my father was obligated to stay with her. That wasn't a problem."

Skylar sat back in her seat and stared at the wipers flinging snow this way and that and tried to imagine months in a hospital with no one visiting. Impossible. She'd be inundated with relatives and school friends. "Do you see much of your dad now?"

"No. I never see him."

"Why?"

"There was just a kind of a mutual agreement not to prolong the agony of our relationship. I don't even know where he lives now."

It was unfathomable. "And the clown you carry?" she asked, her voice very soft.

He spared her a quick glance. "A leftover from childhood."

So he did have some good memories, some connection

to this family of his that apparently hadn't been gifted at parenting.

"It comes from a time before I can remember the people who raised me," he said.

"You mean before your parents?"

The glance he spared her this time was longer. "Yeah." He lifted her hand in his and kissed her knuckles.

"Cole—"

"I see a green turret up ahead," he interrupted. "I think we've found Slovo."

Chapter Ten

Skylar had been one hundred percent right about the hotel. It was like something out of a fantasy or a fairy tale, sitting on an island that wasn't much bigger than it was, reachable only by boat or the narrow bridge connecting it to the town, towers rising to be lost in the snowy skies, secrets lurking in all the shadows. For one minute, as he opened her car door and took her hand to help her out, he wished he could stay with her.

He'd tried, originally, to approach this mission like any other, but now the very idea of that seemed naive. This journey had been fraught with emotional baggage from the get-go. New brothers, a past revealed he'd never guessed at, his own life upside down, what little supposed family he had gone now and out of reach. He'd come here with a personal vendetta, carrying the weight of his brothers' needs as well as his own, and the first thing he'd done was meet Skylar Pope.

And now he wanted to ditch this no-win scenario, seduce the living daylights out of her and spend a little of the inheritance that had showed up courtesy of his brothers. He was getting hedonistic at the ripe old age of thirty.

"I'll be in the hotel somewhere," she said, "but I'd rather you didn't page me. I have my cell phone. Use the phone at the concierge desk to call me."

"Sure," he said.

"This place looks like it'll take what's left of the day to explore."

He handed her the carry-on, and as she took it from him, their hands brushed. In that instant he was transported back to the first time she'd shown up at his hotel room door and he'd kissed her because he needed her to believe he was falling hard and fast for her.

Now he did the same thing, wrapping his free arm around her and pulling her against him, their mouths connecting like fireworks, her lips parting, both of them lost in each other as the snow fell unheeded. But this time, he didn't need to kiss her—well, not for strategy's sake, anyway. This time the need ran deeper and stronger. "Don't go off alone," he said, giving her one last hug. "Stay around other people."

"I'll try."

"And if you get spooked, rent a room and lock the doors, but have someone escort you to the room."

They both looked around at the other guests. Because of the weather, there weren't many braving the outdoors, but those who were didn't look the least bit threatening. Still, when she glanced back at him, he saw he'd reawakened the nerves she'd greeted him with that morning.

"I will," she said. "Don't worry about me."

He left before he could change his mind.

The bridge was partially covered with a long, narrow enclosed building on one side. He'd noticed it when he drove Skylar to the hotel, but this time he found a parking area with five or six cars in it.

The building was empty floor space except for a few benches. The walls were hung with large framed prints of the bridge under construction and looked out toward the hotel through a bank of windows. Of course, the hotel and the island on which it sat were almost invisible now thanks to the falling snow. The room was partially heated but still cool enough to demand a coat. He took a quick perusal of the handful of other people walking from poster to poster, a smattering of different languages reaching his ears.

None of the women wore a green scarf and a black coat. He hoped Irina wouldn't be too late for a host of reasons, starting with his desire to see Skylar again and ending with the difficulty of appearing interested in an exhibit that was worth ten minutes, tops.

A half hour later, it was almost dark outside, and he'd about written her off. She was a cop. Maybe something had happened at work that had held her up. Plus the weather was deteriorating.

He kind of wished he hadn't made Skylar nervous about being followed. She said she wasn't afraid of her uncle—just annoyed at being watched like a kid, but there was something about her reactions to all this that made him wonder. If she truly wasn't frightened, then why all the subterfuge?

As for him, he'd thought he'd shaken off concerns about being followed when they spent all that time in Chiaro looking for the Cazo house. Nobody could have trailed them through the narrow streets that dead-ended without warning. So why had he warned her about going off alone?

It was as though kissing her had awakened instincts he didn't know he had. The thought of something bad happening to her made him shiver inside. And there was only one road in and out of Chiaro. Someone could have easily waited for them at the turnoff and picked them up again when they reemerged.

"Mr. Bennett?"

He turned to find a woman fitting Irina's description. She was younger and prettier than he'd thought she would be, early forties he guessed, with raven-black hair and very pale skin. Her green scarf floated around her shoulders, sparkling with snow.

"Yes, that's me."

"Irina," she said, extending a gloved hand. As they shook hands, she sized him up the way every cop he knew seemed to do. "I'm sorry I'm late," she said at last.

"Don't worry about it. Do you want to talk here or go somewhere else?"

"There's a man who wants to meet you," she said, her voice soft although it seemed to Cole they were the only ones left in the building.

"Who?"

"I don't want to say his name in a public place. He's waiting for us. He's quite elderly and he's still afraid—"

"Afraid? Of what?"

"I'm going to let him tell you. Do you want to ride with me or follow in your own car?"

"I'll follow," Cole said, glancing at his watch. It was almost five o'clock, and the way Irina was acting was just odd enough to make him wary. She took off in a dark red truck—that would be easy enough to follow in the snow.

She led him into the town of Slovo, its narrow cobbled streets crowded with what must be rush-hour traffic. It took several minutes to get to the far edge of town, and then she turned down a road that seemed to skirt the lake. After a mile or so, he began to get nervous about getting stuck out here and wished he'd ridden in Irina's truck, which sat a lot farther off the ground than his rental and probably sported four-wheel drive.

Finally he made out a small house ahead, set off by itself. He parked beside Irina's truck and walked with her to the front door.

It opened as soon as they stepped onto the porch and

an elderly man motioned them inside. He spoke to Irina in his own language, and Cole found himself wishing he could have brought Skylar along because now he was at the mercy of Irina's translations.

He reminded himself his brother John had trusted Irina. He'd lived down the street from her right here in Slovo when he was a kid and had reconnected years later when he'd come to try to understand his past.

"This man's name is Roman," she said, turning to Cole and switching to English. "He doesn't call himself that anymore. Now his name is Tincte, but years ago and in his heart, he is Roman. That's his last name, the only name he needed until this. He's given me permission to tell you that. Does his name mean anything to you?"

"Roman was the last name of the young woman the ambassador supposedly had an affair with and killed."

"Yes. This man is her father and the last remaining member of his family. Two of his sons were murdered many years before by a man your brother John ran into a few months ago back in the United States."

"I know who you mean. Smirnoff. John told me about him."

"Good. You know that John asked me to keep asking questions after he left Kanistan the last time."

"Yes. I know the first time he came here he questioned the people who raised him and that they were murdered when they called Traterg police for help in dealing with him."

"Yes, I discovered that call myself.

"Why did Smirnoff kill Roman's sons?"

"That was the conclusion of the police investigation," Irina added. "Mind you, these are the same police that said Roman and his sons were responsible for the retaliatory bomb that destroyed the ambassador, his wife and their three sons. Roman's own boys were killed, supposedly during an arrest attempt. Roman and his wife got away and have been hiding ever since. He claims they had nothing to do with sending a bomb."

Cole looked closely at the old man as he spoke to Irina. "How did you find this man?"

"I didn't. He found me. His wife passed away recently, and he contacted a trusted friend with the news. That person told Roman I had been asking questions."

The old man touched her shoulder, and she turned to him. He spoke to her in a weedy voice, emotion etching deep lines down his face, bracketing his mouth.

"He's been ashamed," she said, looking back at Cole.

"Ashamed? Why?"

"Because he didn't avenge his children. Because his wife died without her family. Because he lost everything, and to protect what little he had left he changed careers, going from a professor to a fisherman. And because he heard rumors that papers were forged and documents altered."

"Tell him I understand," Cole said gently.

The old man's eyes watered as Irina spoke to him, and he sagged a little. Cole caught his arm and supported him over to a chair pulled up to an old, scarred table.

"If Roman and his sons didn't send the bomb, does he know who did? Does he have any idea who his daughter was really seeing?"

Irina talked to Roman for a few moments, then looked back at Cole. "Yes."

"Will he tell me?"

She spoke to Roman again, sitting back on her heels to get face-to-face with him. The old man looked up at Cole and nodded.

So here it came, the truth at last, handed over like a gift. Cole all but stopped breathing.

"First he wants you to understand the country was in upheaval at the time. There were border disputes, skirmishes and deaths."

"John told me the police chief at the time committed suicide," Cole said. "He was caught in a scandal of some sort."

"That's what the public was told. The truth was the man was murdered to make room for another man."

"Smirnoff."

"Yes."

"Then who really did kill the police chief?"

"Someone committed to owning the police. Someone in the same secret club as Smirnoff."

Cole furrowed his brow. "A secret club?"

"There are old rumors," she said. "I remember my mother talking about them. You've seen the owl ring?"

"Yes." Cole looked out the window at the falling snow and suddenly knew he had to hurry this up before his car got snowed in. He had to see Skylar. He stopped interrupting and sat very still as Irina translated the old man's story.

When he'd heard it all, he got to his feet. He shook the old guy's hand, and Irina walked him to the door. "Can you find your way back by yourself?"

"Yes. You're staying?"

"For a little while. I don't think Roman has been eating much. I'm going to make him something and share it with him. It's hard to eat alone when you're used to sharing meals."

He impulsively leaned over and kissed her forehead. "You're a good woman, Irina.

"Just watch your back."

Cole nodded. It was good advice.

Chapter Eleven

Skylar found a gift shop in a round stone room that looked as though it had once been the dungeon. She only had the lightweight raincoat she'd fled in the night before, and even with her heavy sweater underneath, she was freezing. The castle may have been updated and restored, but it was still a drafty place with cool spots despite the roaring fires and long walkways between buildings.

It had been a long time since she'd actually bought anything retail. Usually she just window-shopped to find inspiration, but this time she went straight to a rack filled with coats, settling at last on an all-weather parka, light blue in color with a white faux-fur fluff around the hood. She hadn't had anything like it in years, not since high school when she'd taken up skiing until she discovered the only sure way to stop—for her—was to fall down.

She bought it on a credit card and folded her own raincoat into the bag the store provided. Nice and cozy now, she walked along the snowy path to the museum, pausing at the pier to look out over the frozen lake toward Slovo, her hair protected from the falling snow.

The pier was built high above the lake with a fifteen-foot drop to the shore and a series of stairs leading down to a dock that would sport a lineup of sail and power boats come summer. The lake wasn't frozen over yet, but it looked as if it was trying, especially close to the shoreline. The shore itself was blanketed with white and with the snow still falling and the temperature plunging, Skylar imagined it would only get more beautiful as the season progressed.

Cole was over there somewhere meeting with a potential supplier. She wished she'd been able to go with him. What a mess she was—how scattered were her thoughts? One minute she was telling him to leave her alone and the next, she was asking him for help. He must think she was nuts.

And yet there'd been moments today when their gazes locked that threw her back to his room, her in his arms, his mouth all over her, warm and moist. All the passion still hung there between them like a gossamer curtain just waiting to be torn down. He'd pulled back that night, and she was ready to talk about it now. He would be leaving Kanistan pretty soon, and who knows how autocratic her uncle would get about her seeing him once she returned to her aunt's side. If Cole left without them coming to some understanding, she might never have the opportunity to know him better, to discover if her feelings were genuine or not, and that struck her as profoundly sad.

That reminded her that she'd asked him to call her when he was ready to meet up again, but she'd turned her phone to silent so she wouldn't have to deal with her uncle. She looked at it now and saw that she'd missed three calls from his private number. Those were three calls she didn't mind missing, yet what if they were about her aunt? What if she'd taken a turn for the worse? How selfish could Skylar possibly bear to be?

She called her aunt, who picked up immediately. "Skylar," Aunt Eleanor said. "I'm so glad to hear your voice."

Hers sounded hollow, and Skylar cringed inside at adding to her worries. "I'm sorry if I upset you by leaving for a little while. I'll be back very soon."

A feeble cough was followed by a deep breath. "Not upset," her aunt said. "It's just been a rough day of treatments. Don't worry about me."

"I guess it was pretty juvenile of me to run off in the dead of the night," Skylar said.

"By the time I knew you were gone, I had your note. I told Luca to get a grip. He treats you like you're twelve."

"He looks out for me kind of like he looks out for you," Skylar said.

"I know. I think he's been calling to apologize and tell you it's safe to come home. He won't lock you in your room."

It was nice that her aunt could make light of it, but right at that moment, after the events of the past twenty-four hours, Skylar found her uncle's controlling nature difficult to bear. But she wasn't going to say that to her aunt.

"Where are you, sweetheart?" Aunt Eleanor asked.

"I don't think I'm going to tell you," Skylar said.

"Are you with Cole Bennett?"

"I'm not going to tell you that, either. Then Uncle Luca can't hum his lullaby and get you to tell him all your secrets."

She managed a laugh.

"Again, Aunt Eleanor, I'm sorry if I caused you a second of alarm. And don't worry. I'll be back by the time the gallery reopens in a couple of days."

Her aunt was quiet for a moment, and when she spoke, it was with a melancholy note in her voice. "Please be kind to your uncle, Skylar. He's under a lot of pressure lately. I know he's worried about so many things."

"I'll try. And I want to assure you I haven't forgotten

your request. I'm still trying to get information about Aneta."

"I shouldn't have asked that of you," her aunt said. "Your uncle and I have always been upfront with each other, and this feels like sneaking around. Poor Aneta was murdered. Snooping could put you in danger, too. Let it go, okay? Leave it to the police."

"Sure, no problem," Skylar said, determined to erase the increased sound of worry from her aunt's voice. They hung up a few minutes later.

So what was gnawing at Skylar's stomach now? Had thinking about Aneta awakened Skylar's memory that Ian Banderas knew Svetlana had tried to kill him? The woman had given Skylar her phone number, and Skylar called it now. Svetlana's voice message answered, and that took the breath right out of Skylar's lungs. She would have bet anything that Svetlana ate, slept and worked with that phone close at hand, worried she might miss a call from her daughter.

Skylar pocketed the phone, and thoroughly chilled now, she hurried along the walkway to the museum. The half-dozen rooms were filled with memorabilia concerning the family that had built the castle and included a small display of clothes collected from the region. Skylar found it warm enough inside to take off her coat. She also found a quiet corner with a bench, took out her sketch pad and started recording the ideas that popped into her head as she gazed at the heavy damask fabrics, beads and pearls and rich colors.

After two hours of this, she flipped through the pages and realized every sketch she'd created was dark and somber, not her usual style at all. She knew it was because her thoughts kept snaking their way back to Svetlana not answering her phone, and she tried calling again. Still no response.

She sat there with her hands in her lap, her thoughts suddenly skipping back to the visit at Aneta's house and the oppressive feeling she'd experienced as the family dynamics played out.

Yelena mourned one daughter and seemingly didn't care about the other's largely unexplained disappearance. She was afraid of her husband but passive. Inna worried about that granddaughter, but her concerns were ignored. Burian apparently terrorized them all. And hovering over everything was the murder of Aneta, who had turned to theft reportedly to save her sister. *Save her from what?*

A dysfunctional family to be sure.

And poor. The furniture and carpet had been worn, old and cheaply made, just like at Svetlana Dacho's place. So both missing girls had come from near poverty. How many more missing teenagers were there that Skylar didn't know about? What was Ian doing with them? Why didn't her uncle know about them?

The woman in charge of the museum came around the corner of a display case and informed Skylar that the museum was closing for the night. Skylar had lost track of time. She hurriedly put her things back in her bag, zipped up her parka and left the museum to discover night had fallen.

The path was abandoned but adequately lit, and the covered portions gave respite from the snow. Skylar began to consider the joys of sitting in front of a blazing fire and sipping something hot, then maybe ordering dinner. Something rich and fattening like cheesy pasta. All of this would be a hundred percent more enjoyable, of course, with Cole sitting across the table, sipping wine with her.

It was getting so late she wondered if he might not suggest taking a room for the night. What would be her response?

Who was she trying to kid? She'd jump on it. She'd jump on him.

What was taking him so long?

Near the pier again, she paused to dig her phone from her pocket to make sure she hadn't missed a call from him or Svetlana. Nothing.

For a moment, she rested her arms on the railing, and like before, she peered toward the hazy lights of the city across the lake. Would she ever come to the Slovo lake area again? Worst case scenario: her aunt didn't make it. Would Skylar continue to come see her uncle? Of course, but not for two weeks at a time. As far back as she could remember, Uncle Luca had worked long hours and seldom been home; without Aunt Eleanor, there would be no reason to stay for extended visits.

But even if, hopefully, Aunt Eleanor did survive, Skylar wasn't a kid anymore, and while helping her aunt was soul satisfying, living under such scrutiny at her house was difficult at best. And there was the matter of time and money, too. Sooner or later, Skylar's fashion career had to take off, didn't it?

Maybe she should try to get on one of those television reality shows and see what happened. A friend of hers from school had done it and enjoyed modest success.

Her uncle would accuse her of daydreaming and in the snow, to boot! She pocketed the phone again, and as she did, she heard the sound of crunching snow and approaching steps.

Expecting to see Cole, she turned quickly, careful of her footing on the snowy pier. The footsteps came closer until a figure appeared out of the dark, but it wasn't Cole.

Skylar wasn't sure how she knew that until she realized there was no limp and the shape was wrong.

And that's when Skylar realized she had done exactly what Cole warned her about doing—gone off alone.

Whoever it was wore a ski mask pulled down over their head and kept coming faster than seemed normal. Confused, Skylar hesitated doing what she wanted to do, which was run back to the museum. The person was close now, carrying something brown and bulky. "Help me," they said, and Skylar stepped forward to see what was wrong. Was there a baby in that blanket?

A swift kick to her knee came out of nowhere. Skylar instantly fell to the pier, but when she looked up at her assailant, all she found was a blanket coming toward her. She raised her hands to push it away, but there was force directing the big cloth, and within seconds, she was trapped.

She fought with the blankct as hands held her down, pushing her all the way to thc pier until her face was laying against the icy wood. She fought for a handhold and attempted to stand, but the surface was slippery. Hands gripped her shoulders and she gasped, instinctively rolling away from her attacker. Blows followed, the person delivering them grunting with the effort. Impulsively, Skylar retreated the only way she could, rolling toward the railing, hoping it was high enough to stop a fall and yet knowing if it was, she'd be trapped.

None of this made any sense.

"Mind your own business," a voice said. It was impossible to separate the hissed words from the repeated blows.

Skylar floundered in the blanket, and then all of a sudden, she plummeted off the edge of the pier and toward the lake. The blanket finally floated from her body. Time stood still for the instant before the jarring crush of the final impact.

How in the world was he going to tell Skylar the truth? Where did he begin? With his own lies and the way he'd used her to arrive at this point? That ought to be a great conversation. He dreaded seeing her again, yet he drove as fast as he dared, burning with the need to share this information despite the devastation that would certainly follow in its wake.

But patience was called for, too. He'd have to find the right place. This whole thing was going to take a while to get through. There were layers to the story. And he knew it was going to frighten and alarm her—break her heart, even. But how could he not be honest with her when if he had his way, the world would soon know the truth about Luca Futura?

This time he used valet parking and entered the hotel lobby, half expecting to find Skylar sitting on one of the velvet-covered sofas that dotted the place. She wasn't there. He checked himself in at the desk because there was no way he could talk to Skylar about this in a public place or in a car where he couldn't look at her and gauge her reactions. This would take privacy, and that meant a room.

Once that was done, he pocketed the key and checked the bar and dining room to make sure she wasn't close by, and then he went to the concierge where he found an English-speaking employee who allowed him access to their phone.

He was startled when she didn't respond. Did she get wind of his real reason for coming? No, that was damn near impossible. Had her uncle's lackey caught up with her and taken her back to Traterg? Now that was more likely. But even if that's what had happened, she'd still have her phone—unless it had been taken from her.

He asked if anyone had left a message for him at the front desk and got a negative.

"I was supposed to meet a woman here." The clerk produced a lecherous smile that Cole ignored. "I can't seem to find her. She's a blonde with some blue in her hair. Anyone fitting that description catch your attention?"

"I have only been on duty a little while, sir," the man said. "I have not seen her."

Cole thought for a moment. "How about directions to the museum, then?"

"I'm afraid the museum has been closed for almost an hour."

"Are there any displays of fabrics or garments in the museum?"

"Yes, sir, but as I said, it's closed."

"She has a way about her. Maybe she sweet-talked the docent into letting her stay a little longer."

The man looked entirely unmoved by this suggestion. Cole got the terrible feeling he was grasping at straws, that Skylar had left the castle, either alone or with someone else. But where did that leave him? How could he drive away from here without at least making sure she wasn't waiting for him somewhere?

"There is a gift shop on the lower floor," the man added as an afterthought. "They have textiles, too, and these are for sale."

"Is it still open?"

The man glanced at the clock. "For another twenty minutes."

Cole followed directions to the lower level, which was filled with various shops and a café. Though it was well lit, the original rough stone walls and lingering aura of the place suggested it was entirely possible he might run into the Count of Monte Cristo at any moment.

The gift shop itself was bright and cheerful and empty except for a single clerk who appeared to be closing up shop. Hoping she spoke English, Cole asked her about Skylar. "About this tall," he said, holding his hand right around his pectoral muscle. "Light hair, blue streak right about here." With that, he touched his head behind his left ear.

"Oh, yes, I remember. Pretty lady. Very young?"

"That's the one. When was she here?"

"Hours ago. Maybe three," she said.

That was soon after he'd dropped her off at the hotel. His initial reaction of excitement faded.

The saleswoman wrinkled her middle-aged forehead as she added, "She buy blue coat, you know, with fur around face. Not real fur. You know."

"I see. Well, thanks for your help."

He searched each of the other businesses that were open with no luck, then climbed the stairs and exited the hotel, zipping his jacket against the sudden drop in temperature. On his way to the museum, he passed a pier that jutted out above the lake. He continued on, winding his way along the walk until it stopped at a locked door. The place was vaguely lit from within but was obviously empty.

It was still snowing but not as heavily as before, and in the better light, he could make out the imprint of footsteps besides his own on the walkway. He followed them back the way he'd come, unsure what to do next. His gut told him Skylar was still here somewhere, but he couldn't make sense out of her not answering her phone. Unless she'd lost or broken it, she had to have it with her.

This time he stopped at the pier because that's where the other footsteps stopped. For a second, he stood there staring toward the distant lights of Slovo, then he caught the glint of gold in the snow. Bending, he retrieved a gold tube that turned out to hold a stick of lipstick.

The color was a shade of red, but whether it was the shade Skylar wore or not, he couldn't be certain. Heaven knows he'd stared at her lips enough today—you'd think he could remember. He was pretty sure the tube itself hadn't been outside lying around for long, and he pocketed it.

Was the snow more disturbed here? Yes, but so what? Maybe kids had come out to play—who knew? He leaned down again to brush some of the newer snow aside, but other than the fact that the lower layer had been compressed, there was nothing to find.

He stood up and turned around, and as he did so, the theme song for *Raiders of the Lost Ark* drifted to his ears. It was so out of place here. Could that possibly be the ring tone for a cell phone, and if it was, could it possibly be hers?

Very unlikely. Why would she choose that music?

Where was it coming from? Grabbing the rail, he leaned over and looked toward the lake, then walked farther out on the pier, trying not to make too much noise lest he miss hearing it again. The lights didn't reveal much down on the shore, but with the coming of the music once again, he was almost positive that's where it came from.

Looking around, he found a set of stairs leading down. A chain closed them off for the winter. He ducked under the barrier and started down the stairs, straining to hear that familiar melody. He did, but by now he was having to feel his way along in the dark as not even ambient light could make its way down under the structure.

He kept waiting for another ring, but it didn't come. The stairs ended abruptly in a deep drift of snow, and though he could see nothing that confirmed Skylar was down here, he called out her name, stopped moving and listened.

His eyes finally adjusted enough that gray became discernable from black. If she'd fallen off the pier somehow, it figured she would have landed near one of the perimeters. Of course, this could be the spot where her uncle's underling caught up with her and she might have lost her phone in a struggle, which would mean Cole was searching for something the size of a pack of cigarettes and for no good reason.

"Skylar," he called, about ready to go back to the hotel and demand the management organize a search party. He could beg, borrow or steal a flashlight and come back and search himself. Even as these thoughts ran through his head, he knew Luca Futura would catch wind very quickly of any trouble, and that would add yet another level of complication and danger.

First things first. *Make sure she isn't down here.*

And that's when he stepped down on something that felt different than snow and just about caused him to lose his footing. He scrambled back and felt around with his hands, standing again with a large piece of what felt like wool. He kept gathering it. A blanket, not wet, just semi-frozen. It didn't feel as though it had been down here long enough to deteriorate.

Because of his injury, his days of falling to his knees were behind him, but he could kneel if he did it carefully, and he did that now, feeling with his hands, extending his reach until he stood up to stretch the damn left leg.

Wait…if she fell she probably survived because of the snow, but that would mean her body's impact would make a hole of sorts. He should be looking for the darkest of the dark spots. He scanned the area closest to where he'd found the tube of lipstick up above, and that's when he finally saw a depression.

Scrambling to the spot, the blanket left behind, he carefully knelt and waved a hand into what felt like a three-foot crater. His frozen fingertips brushed animal fur, and he recoiled for a second until he recalled the description of Skylar's new coat. This time he plunged both hands into the hole and touched a human body.

He immediately began shoveling the snow aside, his hands so cold they lost feeling, his mind on one objective and one objective only. When it felt like he could pull her free, he caught her arms and dragged, and she slid up out of the hole onto the snow. He carefully lifted her torso into his arms, half afraid what revelations the next few seconds would bring.

Was she alive, or was he too late?

Chapter Twelve

Cole lay two fingers against Skylar's icy throat. Her pulse vibrated beneath his pads, and he almost cried out in relief. Laying her limp body back on the snow, he stood up and bent over, leveraging her weight and picking her up in a fireman's hold.

He did his best not to think of the last time he'd carried a human this way. That time it had been one of his fellow soldiers during the battle that had ended Cole's military career. The soldier hadn't made it; he'd been dead by the time Cole reached the relative safety of their bunker.

Not this time. Skylar was alive, and if he had any say in the matter, she would stay alive. He retraced his steps, the light actually better when looking this direction, and slowly made his way back to the stairs. Where was everybody?

He had to get her to the hospital. He could get his car, but that would take time. He had no idea where the nearest hospital was. He should get the front desk to call an ambulance. Delay could cost Skylar dearly, and no matter the consequences, her life was all that mattered.

As he approached the patio outside the main building, she shifted her weight and cried out as if in pain or fear. He'd almost made it inside but stopped immediately and lowered her to a bench that was under an overhang. He sat down beside her, gathering her in his arms.

Terror filled her eyes until he said her name softly and took her freezing hands in his. Blood covered her cheek, ran into her hair, but as her gaze focused on his face and relief flooded her eyes, he knew she was at least thinking straight.

"What happened?" he asked, but she just shook her head, lips trembling, teeth chattering.

"I have a room here. That or the hospital?"

"Room," she managed to mutter.

It took him one second to agree with her. The room was closer, which meant warmth was closer. He stood again and picked her up, this time in a more conventional manner. He carried her inside the hotel, glad the elevators were located on his side of the lobby and he wouldn't have to parade across the open floor. He had the funny feeling there was a story besides an accidental fall, and he was anxious to get Skylar somewhere private and safe where he could defrost her and she could tell it to him.

His own news would have to wait.

Her phone went off again as the elevator rose to the third floor where they disembarked. It must be in one of her pockets. She made no move to answer it or check to see who was calling, nor did he.

"Can you stand?" he asked as they neared his door.

"Y-yes," she said.

He helped her on her feet and kept an arm around her as he used the key card, then as she sagged, picked her up again and carried her inside. The click of the heavy door behind them came as a relief.

He set her down on the padded bench at the foot of the bed. "Take your clothes off, okay?" he said and waited until she nodded before turning up the thermostat, then heading into the bathroom to start the water. The tub was oversize and oval-shaped—a tub meant for two, and he had one jolting moment where he wished things were different.

He returned to find that she'd gone no further than slipping off one shoe. Kneeling in front of her, he removed the other shoe, then gently pulled her to her feet.

The snow had begun to melt, leaving her wet now and visibly shaken. He stripped off her new coat, which had kept her torso dry and probably saved her from hypothermia or worse. Her slacks came next, then her sweater and the blouse beneath until she was standing there in wispy nude underwear. After helping her sit again, he draped a comforter around her then went back into the bathroom and checked the temperature of the water, turned off the tap and returned to the main room.

She'd gotten back on her feet and slipped off her underwear. He stopped short. Up until that second, he'd done his best to regard her as a fellow soldier in trouble, done his best to look past the tantalizing curves and creamy flesh to the human being in need beneath the skin.

But seeing her standing there nude breached all his defenses. There was nowhere to hide from the lust the sight of her generated. Her beauty was fragile, graceful and wonderfully sensual, her body small but lush, breasts modest and perfect, waist tiny and hips curved in a way that jammed his heart in his throat.

She shook her head, and he finally realized she was still shivering and that at least some of that porcelain skin tone was due to the fact she was half frozen.

He put out a hand and she took it. He led her back into the bathroom and helped her into the tub where she sank beneath the water with a tremendous sigh, and he pretended he didn't notice the way her breasts floated.

He grabbed a washcloth, and kneeling beside the tub, he dipped it in the water and used it to wash her face. The cut above her left brow wasn't as bad as he'd feared nor were the other small abrasions, but it looked as though bruises were starting to form on her shoulders and arms. She turned wide eyes up to him. "Did you see…anyone… out there?"

"By the pier? No. What happened, Skylar? Did you fall or what?"

"Someone threw a blanket over me and attacked me," she said, her voice suddenly stronger, but the words still coming slowly. "I rolled off the pier." She tilted her left shoulder forward and twisted her head around as if trying to see something on her back. He took a look for her, again attempting to ignore her physical assets—in this case, the way her back tapered down to her waist and then flared into rounded buttocks below the water.

The sight of a huge bruise near her shoulder blade took off a little of the erotic edge.

"Why didn't they come down after you? Why leave you still alive?"

"It was a warning. They said I should mind my own business."

"Did you recognize the voice or see who it was?"

"No, no. It all happened so fast, and the kicks kept coming."

"Try to put it aside for a minute while you warm up," he coaxed. "Is there anything I can get you?"

"Something warm to drink," she managed to say and then dipped her head beneath the surface. When she sputtered to the top, her wavy hair was plastered to her skull, water cascaded down her face, her fair hair lay across her shoulders. If she didn't look like a mermaid, no one did and no one ever would.

"You're gaping," she said, reaching forward to turn the hot water back on. At least there was finally a trace of the old Skylar in her voice.

"You're gorgeous and you're naked," he explained. "And I'm a man." He touched the blue in her hair and realized for the first time it wasn't real, it was a clip, pinned up under her thick tresses.

"Very clever," he said, opening the clip and pulling the blue strands free. "I thought you dyed your hair a different color every night."

"Now you know the truth."

He set it aside. "If you're sure you're not going to pass out and drown, I'll go order you something. Soup?"

"Soup would be wonderful," she said, lying back in the big tub as steam filled the air around her.

He called housekeeping to come collect her clothes for laundering, then dialed room service. Skylar's phone began ringing again as he hung up the hotel phone, and he quickly dug it out of her coat pocket. The screen identified the caller: Uncle Luca.

What would Luca Futura do if he knew Cole was in a room with his naked niece? How about if he knew someone had attacked her and that the odds were real good it was something Futura had said or done or condoned or whatever that had precipitated it? And what would he say if Cole announced his true last name, the one he hadn't used since he was two years old?

"Was that my phone I heard?" she asked when he returned with news that fortification was on its way.

"Yeah. Your uncle tried to call you."

"He's been trying all day."

"Maybe it's your aunt—"

"I thought of that and called her, but nope, it's just

Uncle Luca wanting me to come home, and I'm not quite ready for that."

"What's with the *Raiders of the Lost Ark* music?"

A fleeting smile crossed her lips. "It's my father's favorite movie. I must have seen it a hundred times. The ring reminds me of him and of home."

"And home reminds you of a time when you weren't involved in murder and attacks."

"I guess. My dad is a great guy. You'll like him. I mean, you would if you ever met him. Not that you will or should or anything."

"Skylar? Calm down. It's okay. I hope I do meet your dad someday. But right now, we have some serious things to talk about."

She sat up, seemed to remember how undressed she was, and slipped lower in the tub. "Can it wait just a bit?"

"Absolutely. But I do think we should alert the hotel."

"About what?"

"You getting attacked on their premises. The police might find something that reveals who did it."

"And then they can call Uncle Luca and get him going on about how dangerous being around you is and upset my aunt in the process? I don't think so."

Face it, he was glad she'd reached this conclusion on her own. No way did he want to give Futura any clue that anything was wrong. He sat down on the edge of the tub, but it was hard to concentrate. When she'd been zombie-like she'd been exquisite and sexy but remote enough where he could separate his feelings for her from his physical reactions. Now that she was starting to move and look and sound like herself, those lines blurred.

"Cole?" she said.

He raised his eyes from her chest and felt like an idiot. "Er, yeah?"

"I see a robe on the back of the door I can use, but did you happen to find my carry-on?"

He'd already stood and moved off, now unable to find a safe place to rest his gaze. "Your carry-on? No. Oh, you mean where I found you?"

"No. On the pier."

"It wasn't up there. Just a tube of your lipstick. Maybe the bag fell with you."

"I know it didn't. I remember landing on it, but that was when I was still on top of the pier. Wait, you found a tube of lipstick?"

"Yeah." He realized he was still wearing his jacket, and he reached into the pocket and brought out the gold tube.

"It's not mine," she said. He opened it and wound out the stick, not exactly sure why he did. "I wear a much lighter shade, and I didn't bring it with me," she added. "That's not mine."

"I found it in the snow on top of the pier. It looks like the color Aneta's mother wore, doesn't it?"

"Lots of women wear that shade," Skylar said, but her voice was subdued.

"I guess another guest dropped it earlier today." He set the golden case on the counter. "By the way, I called housekeeping before I ordered the soup. They're sending up grooming kits for each of us."

A light knock on the outer door followed this announcement. He escaped the bathroom, closing the door behind him, relieved for a few moments to get his emotions—and his body—under control.

"What exactly am I supposed to mind my own business about?" Skylar asked as she stared at the soup. Those hissed words replayed themselves in her head. She could buy being the target of a random act of violence, but what in the world had she done to warrant such a sneaky confrontation?

She'd visited Aneta's family and asked about Aneta's little sister. But how could that possibly be connected to this? Or was it her involvement with Svetlana? Could it have been Ian Banderas who came at her? She frowned in concentration, and her skin prickled. It didn't help that Cole kept glancing at his watch and toying with his food.

And to top it off, she hurt everywhere.

"There was something about the person who attacked me," she said, pushing the half-eaten soup away. Cole, sitting across from her at the room's small round table, set his fork down as though relieved not to have to pretend to eat food he didn't want.

"You said he kicked you once the blanket covered you," he said.

"Over and over again." She stood up, wincing as her weight settled on her left foot. That was the side she'd landed on, and it ached now like she'd been slugged repeatedly with a mallet.

She walked back into the bathroom and returned holding the lipstick tube. "I know what it is," she said.

"It's lipstick," he deadpanned.

"No, what it is about my attacker. I was standing there when I heard footsteps. I thought it might be you, so I turned but realized almost immediately that the size and shape and gait was wrong. The person asked for help, and I thought they might be holding an ill child. A moment later, the blanket came at me. I didn't have time to process it before, but I'm almost positive it was a woman."

"A woman? Really?"

"I think so. And that's why the kicks felt so pointed. It was a woman's shoe instead of a man's. Smaller toe box."

"And that might be why she threw the blanket at you.

If she wasn't that much bigger than you, she might not have wanted to chance getting too close."

"She got close enough to kick the blazes out of my knee. She was strong." Skylar wrapped her arms around herself. The shivers were back as though all the hot water and warm food in the world couldn't reach that frozen, frightened core still inside her.

Oddly enough, a sort of lethargy set in as she stood there, a deep fatigue that spread like creeping tendrils. Cole was suddenly at her side, holding her arms. He looked down into her eyes and she tried to smile, but to her horror what came were tears, quiet ones, sliding down her cheeks, dripping onto her chest where the thick white terry cloth absorbed them.

She tried to explain, but there were no words.

"It's okay," he said, leading her to the bed. He sat down and pulled her onto his lap, wrapping both his strong arms around her. "I think you're having a delayed reaction."

She nodded as the tears kept coming, and for several seconds, they sat there entwined, her crying, him comforting. She'd never felt so sheltered in her life. In that moment, she knew she could trust him, that he wouldn't hurt her, that she was safe with him.

"Any better?" he asked.

She nodded as he handed her a tissue. "I was just so sure it was going to be you, and I was so glad. I wanted to know how your meeting went and have a warm drink together…and then it turned brutal…."

He buried his head against her chest. "I'm sorry it wasn't me," he whispered. "I'm sorry I wasn't there to protect you."

"It's not your fault. You can't always be there for me."

"Can't I?"

She stared into his eyes. "No, sweetheart," she said.

"Life doesn't work that way." She took a breath, trying to gather control over herself. "How did your meeting go?"

"My meeting. Oh. Fine."

"Did it turn out like you wanted? Are you going to buy something from them? Is that how it works?"

He licked his lips. "It's a co-op of women who spin their own wool and create hats and scarves and things. I think it's too small an operation to go global."

"That's too bad." She took another deep breath and added, "You said earlier that you wanted to tell me something. What?"

He searched her face for a moment. "Not tonight."

"Are you sure?"

"I'm positive. Tomorrow morning, okay?"

"Okay," she said.

He finally helped her slide under the sheets. Between the blankets and the thick robe she still wore, the chill began to recede. She curled on her right side and watched him set the room service tray outside the door. The do-not-disturb sign came next. For her part, she never wanted to leave this room again.

Someone was out there waiting for her, waiting for her to stop meddling, stop asking questions although it seemed to her she'd done very little of either. She closed her eyes for a second, putting the fear, the pain and the uncertainty of the past few days aside for a moment, and drifted, the sounds Cole made as he moved around the room comforting to her until sleep swept her away.

HE AWOKE TO a cry. As usual, he was able to instantly go from dead sleep to wide-awake. He found himself in a very plush bed.

Another cry reminded him he wasn't alone, and he turned on the bedside light. Skylar lay facing him, too far away to touch, curled on her side, obviously still asleep but flinching, shoulders twitching, eyebrows furled, lips parting as if in pain.

He scooted across the mattress and touched her arm. It took her a moment, but when she opened her eyes at last, it reminded him of when she'd first come to after the fall: fear followed by relief.

"You're okay," he said. "I'm here."

He'd been inured to terror a long time ago—at least when it came to his own fate. As of today, he knew he could still experience it when it came to her—the thought she was beaten and bruised and frightened made him want to find the jerk behind it and permanently turn off all his lights.

She snuggled into him, her face pressed into his bare chest. When he put his arms around her, he found her robe had come untied. His hands met bare, warm flesh, scented with soap, scented with the essence of her. His head spun as he tried to ignore the physical ramifications of lying with her in this bed in this room, but he was only a man and he'd wanted her for days now.

But he couldn't have her. Not when she was vulnerable like this and not when he had so much to tell her that would probably forever color the way she thought about him. He tried to withdraw his arms, but she grasped him tighter.

"Don't leave me," she said, her breasts pressed against his chest, warm and weighty and delectable, her breath hot against his throat. She titled her face up and looked into his eyes.

"Kiss me," she said.

"I can't." He whispered it but it sounded like a blast from a bazooka.

"You want me," she said, kissing his neck, her hands in his hair, running along his shoulders.

"God, yes," he said.

"Then take me."

He found her lips and kissed her. There was no need to tease her lips apart. Her mouth was open, and the touch of her tongue against his shot through his body like a cattle prod. For a moment, he lost his head. Skylar was all there was in the world, all he wanted. He didn't want revenge, he didn't want justice, he didn't want brothers or even tomorrow. All he wanted was her.

"I can't," he said, coming up for air as his hands cupped her breasts and his mouth longed to follow.

"Why? Were you hurt…there…too?"

"No," he said.

She touched his rock-hard maleness, and a chuckle sounded from deep inside her. "I didn't think so," she said. "I take the pill. It's safe."

"It's not any of that," he said, though talking was damn near impossible as she hadn't stopped touching him. "Skylar, please."

Her gaze was suddenly riveted to his again. "No. You listen to me. Unless there's a wife at home you neglected to mention, I don't want to hear it right now. Okay?"

He kissed her lips again, sucking on the lower one. He'd make a meal out of her if he could. "Are you sure?"

"Oh, yes," she said as her head disappeared down his body, kissing him as she went until her lips touched his erection, and he almost shot through the roof. He immediately pulled her back up beside him. He didn't want it to end too quickly especially since she was obviously as aroused as he was. Her nipples were hard beneath his fingertips, begging to be sucked.

"I love you," she said softly, and that caught him off

guard. He could think of nothing to say that wouldn't compound his duplicity, so he kissed her instead, long and deep, his burning need for her turning him inside out.

He'd come so close to losing her.

He clutched her soft, naked rear and pulled her against him. As he lowered his head to devour her luscious flesh, he knew there was only one way for this night to end. Tomorrow would come soon enough.

Chapter Thirteen

Skylar awoke to find herself alone in the huge bed. She spent a moment stretching and yawning and reliving the exquisite sensations that had kept her awake half the night. Cole Bennett was a hell of a lover. She wasn't exactly a pro when it came to sex, but she knew enough to know when a man was selfish and when he was innately generous, and Cole was generous, seeing to her needs before his own.

She sat up at last and found the bathroom door open. Until that moment, she'd assumed he was in there, but now it was clear the room was empty. Where could he have gone? She got out of bed and slipped back on the heavy robe before noticing her clothes from the day before were now draped across a chair, encased in laundry bags, looking clean and pressed. Her shoes were even polished. She took everything into the bathroom and emerged a few minutes later, dressed and suddenly ravenous.

Cole was just coming through the hall door, carrying her carry-on in his hands. He smiled when he saw her, a smile that lit every inch of his face. She hurried to his open arms, lifting herself on her tiptoes and kissing his cheek. "Good morning," she whispered.

He embraced her, kissing her forehead in a fierce, almost defiant manner. His skin was cold and a little ruddy. "Where did you find that?" she asked, glancing at her bag. He looked so strong and so very male, her opposite in many ways. She yearned for him to pick her up and carry her back to the bed.

"Stuffed in a garbage can," he said. "I went to the pier and looked around. It appears someone came back during the night and evened everything out. The depression you made when you fell has been covered and all our tracks obliterated both on top of and under the pier."

Whatever peace she'd been able to find that morning now fled. Someone had come back. Was their intention to finish her off? Had they had second thoughts about leaving her alive? She dropped her arms and stepped away from him, the room suddenly a sanctuary she was afraid to leave.

"I should've staked it out," he added. "I might have been able to catch whoever is behind this."

Was that why he was acting odd, because he'd allowed himself to go to bed with her instead of sitting in the cold all night to catch a bad guy?

"Let's order breakfast from the room service menu," she said.

"I already did," he replied, taking off his jacket. "I have something to talk to you about before we head back to Traterg."

"That sounds serious," she said lightly, but her words landed like a brick in a punch bowl. He only nodded. Her stomach clenched; her appetite disappeared. Nevertheless, breakfast showed up a few minutes later. Cole met the waiter at the door and sent him away, rolling the tray of covered dishes into the room himself.

They sat at the round table again and picked at eggs and fruit. He could hardly meet her gaze, and that alone disturbed her.

"This is about last night, isn't it?" she said.

He looked up from studying a strawberry. "Yes."

"I'm sorry."

"What are you sorry about?"

"I shouldn't have mentioned love. It's too early. I said you were going too fast and then I blurted that out. Don't feel bad because you don't care for me that way. I was just caught up in the moment."

"Stop," he said, laying his fork down on his plate. "This has nothing to do with that. Your telling me you love me did not upset me. Quite the contrary. Let that go."

"What then?" she asked, getting to her feet. She crossed to the window and looked down at the castle grounds. All she could think about when she looked through the window were snipers on the battlements looking up at her. She moved away.

"I need to talk to you about my meeting last night."

She tilted her head. "Okay." She waited as he wandered over to the window and stared outside, a knot in his jaw. "You told me a little bit about it already," she reminded him.

"Yeah. Well—" he turned around and pinned her with his intense blue gaze "—it wasn't actually a business meeting."

She sat down on the bench at the foot of the bed. "What kind of meeting was it?" she asked.

"Personal."

"Oh." What she didn't add was *I knew he was hiding something! What is it? A wife or a child or heaven forbid, both?* "So it wasn't the main reason you came to Kanistan?" she asked, hopeful he could reassure her.

"It's exactly why I came," he said.

So much for hope. "You're confusing me."

"I'm not here for the import/export business."

"I figured that. But you're legitimate. Uncle Luca checked you out."

"Yes, it's a legitimate business and I'm part owner, and it's true I've only been doing it a few weeks. But that's a cover for the real reason I'm here, which, as I said, is extremely personal."

She wished he would just say whatever it was he had to say. "And the real reason you're here is to do what exactly?"

He crossed the room and sat next to her on the bench, his hands folded in his lap. No parts of their bodies touched, and that in itself struck Skylar as ominous. "You're scaring me, Cole," she added softly.

"I apologize for that. You know, this might be easier if I told you a little more about myself."

"Yes," she said, detecting a tremor in her voice.

"First off, I was adopted. I didn't know anything about it until after my adoptive mother died. What I told you about my adoptive father is true. We did not have an easy relationship, and I guess I now understand why.

"When I was about two years old, my birth parents were killed and my two older brothers were adopted out to different families. So was I. The family that took me originally, however, had health and financial troubles and couldn't keep me so they released me. I was adopted by the people who raised me."

"That must have been very hard for them and for you."

"I don't recall any of it, but according to my adoptive father, I cried pretty much all the time. It turned him off completely, and he washed his hands of me. My adoptive mother was different. She was a kind woman with a million causes pulling her a million directions, but she'd never been around children, and then she got stuck with a traumatized toddler. Hardly the cozy scenario she'd pictured. Anyway, because of the two families, I ended up with a different last name than the people who arranged the adoption originally knew about."

"Does that matter?"

"Yes. But first things first."

"How did your parents die?" she asked. There was a part of her that was so relieved this didn't have anything to do with her that she was beginning to relax. Whatever his problem was, she would be there for him and help him fix it. She leaned forward, anxious now to understand.

"They died in a fire."

"That's terrible!"

"They were murdered. Someone didn't want my father to act on information he had that would have landed them in jail and ruined their career for good. So they killed him and my mother, too. Then they framed another man's family, killed half of them and ran the others underground."

"This sounds like the plot for a movie," she said.

"I know, but it actually gets worse. This person was responsible for the well-being of my brothers and myself should something happen to our parents, so they had total control. After the explosion, this guy and his cohort spread the story that the children had died, too. The oldest one had been injured and his memory affected, so they kept him close by, but the two little ones—and that includes me—got sent off to the United States with forged documents and passports and adopted out to unsuspecting families."

"You were separated from each other," she said, holding her stomach, her thoughts flying to her siblings. "Does this mean you know where your brothers are now?"

"It does. They managed to find me with the help of the woman I met with yesterday."

"And your brothers told you all of this?"

"They want justice for our parents and for themselves. The older one, John, especially suffered because of this."

"But what about the police? Surely they can reopen the case."

"The police were in collusion back then, and there's every reason to suspect they are now, too. For instance, when John came back here to find out about his past, the people who raised him were murdered for speaking with him, and every indication is that it was the police who were behind it. John actually came face-to-face with the man who orchestrated that part of the cover-up."

"Came back here? You're from Kanistan originally?"

"No, my father worked here. He was an American. And yesterday I met the last member of the family that was wrongly accused of killing him. The old guy doesn't have anything to live for anymore, which means he doesn't have much to lose. He wanted me to know the truth. He told me the name of the man who did all this."

She sat back on the bench. "Who is it?"

He stared deep into her eyes. "Skylar, I'd give anything in the world if I didn't have to tell you this."

"Who?" she demanded, her stomach now halfway up her throat.

He whispered the name. "Luca Futura."

She sat there staring at him, trying to make sense of one thing he said, *anything* he said. "You're mistaken," she finally said on an exhaled breath that emptied her lungs.

He took her hands in his. "My father was Charles Oates. Ambassador Oates. And your uncle was his right-hand man here in Kanistan—not an American but a trusted ally and friend."

She pulled back her hands and covered her ears. Before she knew it, she was standing. The room, which had seemed a sanctuary moments before, now resembled a trap.

Her hands fell to her sides as her mind raced to keep up with a million questions, all coming too fast to make sense.

"He betrayed everyone, Skylar. He got a girl pregnant then had her murdered."

"No!" she said. "The ambassador is the one who did that. My uncle had just married Aunt Eleanor—"

"Which is probably why he panicked."

"You're wrong, Cole. I know you are."

"Just listen to me. Roman, I mean the girl's father, went to my dad when he found her body." He shook his head. "I shouldn't have said that name though I can't see why it matters. Just don't repeat it. Few people know he's still alive. Anyway, this man pointed a finger at your uncle. He'd seen Luca with his daughter. He knew. But even then, Futura was not a man to be crossed. The girl's father asked my father to help him find justice. My father agreed to talk to Luca that very night while his family was away—at the circus, no less. But we came home early because I ate too much junk food and got sick. Futura had no intention of facing murder charges. By then he owned the police chief, and the two of them cooked up this plan. They delivered a bomb to our house.

"What neither one of them knew was that Tyler—he's the middle brother—had decided to return to the circus by himself and crawled out his window. Once he got outside, the darkness scared him so he hid beneath the bushes. He heard someone whistling and recognized the tune as one his father's friend often hummed. It was coming from the other side of the fence where your uncle was keeping watch while the bomb was taken to our door. It was disguised. My other brother, John, remembers thinking the box was for him, a present. Anyway, before Tyler could do much of anything, there was an explosion. The crooked cop belonged to some old club of conspirators who used to run things here. Their symbol was an owl ring—"

"This is crazy!" she cried. "Crazy." She paced up and down the room, the large muscles in her legs begging for more. She wanted to run—run hard and fast and away.

And then she stopped and stared at him. "You've been lying to me since the day you walked into my aunt's gallery, haven't you?"

He looked from her face to the floor. "Yes."

"You knew about her illness, didn't you?"

"Yes."

"And you chose me because you thought I would give you an in to my uncle."

"Yes." He looked up at her, his eyes pleading with her to understand.

Oh, she understood, all right. "That's why you kissed me. That's why you came on so strong and fast."

"Yes. And no, Skylar."

"Which is it?"

"Yes, I used you. No, it wasn't all just that. It never was, not from the moment our eyes met."

"Oh, my God. I told you I loved you. That must have been the icing on the cake."

"No, Skylar, it's not like that. You and I—"

"There is no you and I," she said. She didn't believe him. He'd conned her. Her voice dropped as her eyes widened. "Did you have something to do with Aneta's murder?"

He got to his feet, and as he stepped toward her, she backed away. "Of course not."

"Did you arrange that attack on me?"

"Skylar, please."

"Well, think about it. How better to worm your way into my uncle's graces than to save me—again? Is Svetlana also part of your scheme? Is that why she's not answering her phone?"

"Just stop a minute. I don't know Svetlana. As far as I know she's exactly who and what she appears to be. If you'll just listen. I've been thinking about what the man I met last night said about how your uncle forged papers and passports. What if that's what's happening with these girls who are missing? That would make the whole 'going to America' thing make sense. What if they're being shipped overseas? Sold, maybe?"

"I suppose my uncle is behind that, too?"

"I think so."

She stared at him with her mouth open. She'd read about people having out-of-body experiences. Perhaps this was what it was like. Watching things unfold, impossible things that could destroy everyone she cared about and not finding one thing to say or do to put a stop to it. "Why should I listen to you?" she asked at last.

"Because you know in your heart that I care for you. You know most of what's happened between us is as real as the air we breathe."

"No, I don't," she said. "What I know is you conned me into trusting and needing you so that you could live out some fantasy to clear a family name you don't even use and ruin the life of a good man with a very ill wife who needs him. When I think of how stupid I've been! How delusional! I should have listened to Uncle Luca."

The back of her nose burned with unshed tears. She did not want to show one ounce of weakness to this man, this stranger.

"Then what about the girls?" Cole asked. "What about

Zina and Malina and maybe even the other one, Katerina?"

"What about them?"

"Where are they? Why did Aneta risk everything to try to get her sister back? Who killed her for her efforts?"

Skylar rubbed her eyes. Her throat ached with the emotion she strove to keep inside, out of view. She'd been headstrong and gullible, a deadly combination. She narrowed her eyes and planted her hands on her hips. "I don't know what's real or not. I don't know that anything I thought happened actually happened. I know Aneta is dead and that she stole a painting, and I know that you are a conniving double-crossing jerk. I don't know if your story is real, if you're adopted or have brothers or have ever been in the military or who your parents really were. All I know for sure is you picked what you determined was the easiest way to get close to my uncle so that you could do whatever it is you want to do. And I was the idiot who let you."

He rubbed his temple with the heel of his hand. "I didn't have to tell you any of this. I could have just done what needs to be done and gone my merry way and you never would have known."

"And I wish you had," she said.

"Do you? You think a man capable of destroying people, of murdering his pregnant mistress, of manipulating the police and being involved in trafficking human beings—"

"That again!"

"If your uncle could forge identities thirty years ago for me and my brothers, he can do it now."

"If that's true, it's Ian Banderas's doing."

"Do you really think Banderas could get away with a scheme like that without your uncle's knowledge?"

"Of course, he could."

"No, Skylar. He couldn't."

"Why do you hate Uncle Luca so much? Is it because you can't face what your father did?"

He took a deep breath. When he looked at her, she had to glance away. "You refuse to listen. I told you that the man whose daughter was murdered didn't send the bomb. He was framed, his sons killed during their supposed arrest."

"You want me to believe hearsay and the story of a complete stranger and disbelieve a man I've known my whole life. I can't do that."

He walked up to her and she backed away, unwilling to be close to him, but that ended when she bumped into the wall and had to stop. He loomed above her, his arms extended, his hands against the walls at either side of her head. "I want you to keep an open mind."

"That's ripe coming from you," she said.

"I know you don't want to face what he is. I don't blame you."

"You don't blame me?" She ducked under his arm and walked away.

"Skylar?"

She whirled around. "I don't know who you really are. I only know from this minute on that I never want to see you again. I'll call my uncle to come get me or arrange transportation. I hope I'm making it very clear that I'm asking you to have nothing to do with me or any of my family."

"I can't do that," he said. "I can't let Futura get away with this."

"You came here with your mind made up."

His face grew rigid. "Do you think it gives me any joy to tell you these things? And do you think I went through all this on a whim? All the leads have led my brothers and the police officer they're working with here to this man. The story I just told you is true. It's a composite of what many people have unearthed. Tyler even had himself hypnotized in order to recover his lost memories. At the very least, your uncle's past has to be investigated, and frankly, I don't care how you feel about that."

"What about my aunt?"

"I'm terribly sorry for her. If she really doesn't know the kind of man she's married to, this is going to be awful. You and she will be yet another family he's destroyed, but at least you'll have each other."

"You're doing the destroying now."

"And you're allowing your own self-interests to blind you to the truth."

"And you're not?"

His eyes hardened. "There's nothing left for us to talk about." A muscle worked in his jaw, and he added, "I doubt you really want to wait here for hours while someone comes to get you. You're welcome to come with me. I'm going to go settle the bill and get the car. Make up your mind. Your decision."

And with that, he left the room.

THEY DROVE IN SILENCE colder than the icy snow outside.

Cole had often felt alone in his life but never really like this. He'd always been self-reliant, able to lead or follow depending on the situation and his orders, but a loner at heart. Last night he'd connected with another human being in a way he'd only read about, only half understood. Last night he finally "got" it. And it wasn't about sex— well, not entirely. It was so much more than that.

He'd always assumed the idea of a soul mate, someone destined to be yours, someone who would love you no matter what, was a fairy tale, but last night he'd stumbled into that dream right there with Skylar. Finding her in the snow, scared she'd never wake up again, helping her bathe. And then later… Well, he'd do anything to keep her safe.

Anything except walk away from what had to be done.

But none of her reactions came as too big of a surprise. He'd known all along there was going to be a stiff price to pay for growing attached to her. Of course she thought he was a louse who had used her for his own means. And in so many ways, she was right—he had.

She didn't say a word until they were almost to her uncle's place. Then she turned in her seat but averted her glance. "Stop here."

He pulled over to the curb. They were three or four blocks away. She grasped the door handle but before working it spoke again. "What are you going to do?"

"I'm going to go public," he said. The idea just popped into his head, but it stuck there. "I'm going to talk to anyone who will listen to me. I'm going to crush this man just as he's crushed everyone I care about—and that includes you."

"You won't let the past go?"

"You still don't get it. I believe this is ongoing. But in all fairness, you're right. I do aim to settle the past, as well. You were all for that until you realized who was responsible."

"This will destroy my aunt. Even if it isn't true, she won't live through the scandal. You're wrong about my uncle, and I'm going to prove it."

He reached for her hand. "Don't try to prove anything. He's dangerous."

"Listen to yourself. He's my uncle!"

"Then think beyond that. Think beyond him. Think of the other people he's harmed."

She stared hard at him. "You do the same," she said. "If you're going to ruin him and half my family along with him, then at least have solid proof beyond the word of an old man who could have a whole other agenda you don't know a thing about."

"Like what?"

"Like clearing his name before he dies. Like getting back at my uncle because of a reason you don't know."

He sat back in his seat. Had he been so willing to believe the worst that he'd sacrificed judgment?

She pulled free and got out of the car, stuffing her hands in her pockets and walking away without looking back, a slight figure, no bigger than a schoolgirl.

She was no longer his. Truth was, she'd never been his.

Chapter Fourteen

Skylar used the security code to let herself in the front door of her aunt and uncle's house. Not even the butler greeted her, and she was relieved. She desperately needed a few minutes alone as the past few hours had been hell. She would retreat to her room and collect herself before putting on a brave face for her aunt and deciding what to do about Cole.

The one and only issue that concerned her now was how much she should tell her uncle of what Cole had said about him. The prospect of that conversation made her stomach roll over and sink. And the fact she would have to admit she'd played right into Cole's hands was like admitting she threw the first punch.

She escaped upstairs where she applied a little makeup to cover the scratch on her forehead. Then she went directly to her aunt's room where she found her sitting up in bed eating a small meal.

"I'm glad you've come home," Aunt Eleanor said, her wan face pleased.

"How are you?"

"Okay. Have you seen your uncle?"

"Not yet."

"You will talk to him, won't you?" she asked, her voice revealing how deeply she wanted them to get along.

"Of course I will."

"He only has your best interests at heart. I know this about him. Family is everything. If you are his, he will do whatever it takes to protect you."

"Don't worry," Skylar assured her, but her aunt's words just made her more uneasy than ever. She didn't want her uncle to protect her at the expense of hurting Cole.

"Meanwhile, guess what?" her aunt continued and when Skylar shook her head, she continued, "An old friend of mine heard what happened to Aneta and knew I would be shorthanded. She just retired a few months ago. She owned a stationery store. Anyway, she has offered to take over the gallery until I am well enough to come back. Her daughter is going to help out."

"That is great news," Skylar said.

"I couldn't believe it. I know Luca thinks it's time we let you get back to your own life in the States. I couldn't agree more. Now you can."

Skylar felt a wave of relief and an equal one of disappointment. It was hard to believe that she'd had everything she ever wanted just twelve hours before and now it was all gone. "Let me tell you about the museum I visited," she said, determined to wash away the worry lines creasing her aunt's brow.

Halfway through the recital, her food barely touched, her aunt fell asleep. Skylar left the room quietly.

Downstairs, she found her uncle standing at the open front door. He closed it immediately when he heard Skylar behind him. "I'm glad to see you've come to your senses," he said. "Have you seen your aunt?"

"I was just with her. I need to talk to you, Uncle Luca."

"Let's go into the den," he said, leading the way across the foyer. Skylar glanced out the bank of windows and saw a man walking away from the house. The wind tousled his blond hair.

Ian Banderas. At the house—again. "What was he doing here?" she said, pausing to stare after Banderas.

"I beg your pardon?" her uncle said.

"Ian Banderas. I thought you didn't like him coming to the house."

The look he cast her made Skylar back off. "I'm sorry if I sound like an inquisition," she said.

"Come in here a moment," he replied, and they continued into his office.

After sitting behind his desk, he steepled his hands together and rested his chin on his fingertips. "Things have gotten rather…awkward between us as of late," he said.

She glanced behind him at the wedding portrait of him and her aunt. "Tell me about your ring," she said, eyeing the gold and black encircling his finger both in the painting and in real life. She'd always just assumed it was a keepsake of some kind, not some symbol of dark intent.

"The owl? They're amazing birds, you know. They hunt by stealth and surprise, almost blind when it comes to something very close by but extremely adept at long-range vision. They blend in. They usually operate under the cover of darkness. There's a lot to admire about an owl."

Skylar had remained standing, the thought of sitting and chatting at odds with the anxiety spitting acid in her gut. She paced a little before asking, "Does Ian Banderas have a ring like yours?"

He appeared surprised by her question. "Of course not."

"I heard the ring was once a symbol of a secret club."

"Oh, that. Someone has been filling your head with old rumors. Yes, once upon a time a few of us had a club, but that was the old days. I'm the only one left."

She couldn't bring herself to accuse him of the things Cole said he did. If he was innocent, she would forever damage their relationship. If he was guilty, what was the point?

"I think I can guess who's been talking to you," he said, his voice crisp with disapproval. "Cole Bennett."

"Cole Bennett is no longer in the picture," she said.

He narrowed his eyes as he studied her. "What happened to your face? Did that man strike you?"

"No, nothing like that." She paused before adding, "Uncle, what can you tell me about your old friend, Ambassador Oates, and his family?"

Irritation curled his upper lip. "No, Skylar, I am not going to discuss the past with you. It's water under the bridge, best left alone."

"But please. There was another family, too, right? I mean, the murdered girl's family. They were hell-bent on revenge. Isn't that what you said? They sent a bomb—"

"I am not—repeat, not—going to talk about the Roman clan. They're all dead and gone. Good riddance to them."

Roman. That's the name Cole had mentioned then asked her not to repeat. "What if it isn't? What if the girls I keep telling you are missing—"

"Girls? There is more than that one unfortunate waif?"

"I found out Aneta's sister is missing under similar circumstances and that Ian Banderas was known to her family."

He shook his head. "I asked you to let the police take care of this. I told you I would talk to Ian."

"What did he say?"

"Just what I suspected. Malina Dacho was an opportunistic cheat. Plain and simple. They come and go, these girls. They run off. They put themselves in harm's way.

In this case, the mother is trying to extort money from anyone who will listen to her story and fall for her lies."

Skylar stared at her uncle and tried to connect the girl Svetlana believed her daughter to be with the girl her uncle just described. And this glib response didn't explain the money she'd left behind, either.

At least Ian had confirmed he knew of Malina Dacho, which meant Cole hadn't created that situation to advance his plan. So why wasn't Svetlana answering her phone?

"Again," her uncle said, "I'm asking you what happened to your face? There are scratches on your arms, as well."

"I was attacked by a woman," she said.

He stood abruptly. "What?"

"A woman threw a blanket over me and kicked me. I fell, but I'm okay—just a little sore and battered. Someone doesn't want me asking questions."

"That does it," he said. She'd never witnessed his eyes so narrow or his nostrils as flared. "Your aunt has an offer from an old friend willing to take care of the gallery. I'm seeing to it that you go home as early as next week, and until then, please confine yourself to this house. I have calls to make now. You may go."

SKYLAR GRABBED HER red coat from the downstairs closet and left the house before her uncle could bar her way. More than ever, she wished she could talk to Cole. The conversation with her uncle had left her confused and nervous. Ian Banderas, who days before hadn't been welcome in her aunt and uncle's home, was now there frequently. Why?

Could Cole be right?

It took her a few tries with a patient cab driver to find the neighborhood she'd gone to just once—and then in the dead of night with Svetlana giving directions. The house itself turned out to be easy to identify as there were two ambulances and several police cars pulled up outside and what appeared to be a television news crew unloading their gear.

Skylar paid the driver and hurried toward the gathering crowd. She caught a glimpse of Detective Kilo at the door and ducked behind a tall man carrying a tiny camera, stepping on his foot in the process. He looked down at her in surprise. "Sorry," she said.

"No problem," he replied. With a sweeping gesture that took in the house, he added, "This is all so sad."

"What happened?" she asked, dreading the answer.

"Two women died," he said.

"What!"

"All I know is what the woman who found the bodies told me," the man said. "She's right over there." He pointed at an elderly woman in a very large black coat and scarf who stood off by herself next to a police car. "She went there today like she does every morning to have coffee with Rita Guro. That's whose house this is. Was. Poor Mrs. Kintz is really shaken."

"I think I'll go console her," Skylar said. "Thanks."

She made her way to the woman who watched her approach with solemn eyes. "I'm sorry about your friend," Skylar said by way of greeting.

The woman shook her head. "It was terrible. Why would Svetlana do such a thing?"

No, no, no.

"They were both seated at the table, just as I left them yesterday afternoon," Mrs. Kintz continued, "with their mending supplies all set out in front of them, normal as can be. In fact, Rita still held a needle in her hand. But half her head was gone, blown away." Mrs. Kintz paused to chew on a knuckle and choke back fresh tears. "Svetlana must have shot her from behind. At least Rita didn't know it was happening."

"But how do you know it was Svetlana who murdered her?"

"The gun was in her hand," Mrs. Kintz said. "It looked like she shot Rita, then calmly sat down across the table from her and shot herself. There was blood everywhere. I just met her yesterday. She did not seem the kind of person to do something so evil."

Skylar fought to make sense of this, but she couldn't. "Look, they're coming out," the older woman added.

Skylar turned as two gurneys, each carrying a body bag, appeared in the doorway. Attendants rolled them to separate ambulances.

"The police say they've been dead since yesterday, but I don't understand," the woman said. "When I left them, they were telling stories as they did the mending. In fact, Rita was still holding the blue dress she was working on when I left. Svetlana got a phone call that seemed to upset her and said she would be leaving soon. What could have gone so terribly wrong in such a short time? Svetlana must have been crazy."

"Where did she get the gun?" Skylar asked. "Did Rita have one?"

"Oh, no, she lost two sons in wars. She wouldn't have a gun anywhere near her. Svetlana must have brought it."

But Skylar knew Svetlana didn't have a gun, or if she did, she'd certainly not had the opportunity to pack it before she and Skylar left her apartment in such a hurry. It didn't add up. Surely the police would figure this out.

Or would they? Cole said they were corrupt.

Skylar squeezed the woman's arm gently. "I really am sorry for your loss," she said. A couple of policemen were looking her way, so she hurried off down the sidewalk, heedless of direction, desperate to get away.

She knew three things. One was that she was responsible for both these deaths. By telling her uncle who then told Banderas, she'd as good as pulled the trigger.

She also knew Svetlana hadn't killed her friend. It made no sense. If the police announced they believed this story, then Cole was right: they were involved in a cover-up.

The other thing she knew was that Cole was in danger. Ian Banderas had either killed Svetlana or had her killed just hours after her uncle talked to him. Now her uncle would talk about Cole. Cole would be next.

She had to warn him. She pulled out her phone and called the hotel, asking for his room.

"I'm very sorry," the desk clerk said, "but Mr. Bennett checked out an hour ago."

Skylar clicked off the phone and kept walking.

Now what?

Chapter Fifteen

Cole felt eyes trained on the back of his head.

He turned quickly, glancing behind him. and found a man gazing placidly back, thick lips slack, totally disinterested.

Cole had just dropped his rental off at the airport and was now on the transport bus to the terminal. He knew Traterg had added additional flights to America recently, and there was one leaving around 1:00 a.m. He'd be lying if he didn't admit how much he wanted to be on it. For the first time in his life, he had family he wanted to spend time with, yet he had a profound premonition in his gut that would never happen. Just as a future with Skylar was now out of the question.

Her last words to him played through his mind and the thing was, she was right. He'd been willing to take Roman and Irina at face value. He needed proof of some kind before mounting any campaign; that need was what had brought him here, and he mustn't lose sight of it. But his time in Kanistan was running out.

By now, Skylar must have told her uncle everything Cole had told her, and he was a sitting duck. Even the United States might not be far enough away. And without Skylar by his side, without the promise of the days and weeks and years of growing old with her, what did any of it matter, anyway?

Well, he hadn't been a soldier for years for nothing. This was the time to draw on cunning and guile, to trust in the purpose of his mission and rededicate himself to its conclusion. He knew in his heart that Futura was behind the deaths of his parents, the deaths of John's guardians and, undoubtedly, the deaths of many others. Enough was enough. Without Skylar as a distraction, he could get back on track, figure out the next step. She, at least, would be safe with her uncle, and that was really all that mattered.

The bus stopped and he got off. The man who had been sitting behind him got off as well. Cole retrieved his luggage from the back of the van and tucked his briefcase under his arm as he made his way inside the terminal. He lost the man from the bus in a crush of people and breathed a little easier.

It took no time at all to check in for the flight thanks to purchasing a first-class ticket. Now he just had to wait several hours for the plane to take off and he would be free.

He had just entered the bathroom to splash cold water on his face when he spotted the reflection of the man from the bus in the mirror. The dispassionate look on his face was nowhere to be seen; now there was an expression of intense concentration. Cole took a hasty look around. The bathroom was depressingly empty, and the only way out was through the man.

Holding his briefcase in front of him, Cole turned abruptly. The guy jammed his big body against Cole just as another man came into the room. A moment's relief was followed by the realization that the new man was working with the first guy. He came up behind Cole, who caught the glimmer of steel in the reflection. He pushed forward as hard as could while spinning his body out of the way right as the second man lunged with a knife.

The blade missed Cole but entered the first man's throat. Blood immediately spurted like a geyser as the victim fell heavily to the tiled floor. The second guy immediately set upon ripping his knife from the neck of the dead man, but Cole didn't wait around. He took off at a brisk walk that quickly grew faster, shrugging himself out of his overcoat and tossing it onto a row of empty chairs. The briefcase miraculously remained in his hands. Behind him, he could hear the pounding of footsteps....

EVENTUALLY SKYLAR STOPPED to look around to see where her feet had carried her. She found she'd entered a neighborhood that appeared to be transforming itself from squalid to quaint. What looked like new shops appeared more and more frequently. Small restaurants and bakeries occupied almost every corner.

She saw the sign for Pushki's café from across the street and paused. What was the name of the girl who had been Malina's friend? Skylar couldn't remember but never mind: fate had brought her to the place Malina supposedly met Ian Banderas; Skylar might as well find out what she could.

She entered the café slowly, waiting for her eyes to adjust to the dim light. It was a moody-looking place with cigarette smoke heavy in the air giving the impression the real action started after the sun went down. What was a fifteen-year-old doing working in a place like this?

Probably trying to help her mother keep a roof over her head...

And now her mother was dead....

A girl approached with a menu, but Skylar wasn't interested in eating and declined being seated. She remembered Svetlana had mentioned a friend of hers who was a dishwasher here, but for the life of her, she couldn't think of a way to ask after the kitchen help. Back on the street, she got the idea of finding the alley behind the restaurant. Once she'd located that, she made her way to what appeared to be the kitchen door.

Two men were in the process of unloading cases of liquor from a van while another man marked the items off on a checklist. Skylar asked the man with the list if she could speak with the dishwasher. He waved her inside without even looking at her.

The kitchen was very small and cramped. A thin man poaching fish glanced at Skylar without interest. She smiled and sidled past him to approach a back room from which steam billowed forth.

The dishwasher turned out to be a round-bellied guy of about fifty with curly gray hair and large bags beneath his eyes. Skylar asked him if he knew Svetlana Dacho, and he stared at her as though trying to figure out her angle.

He must have decided she looked harmless because he told her to come with him. They walked back through the kitchen and out the door, past the liquor transaction and stopped near a stack of crates. The dishwasher took out a pack of cigarettes and perched himself on a box. He offered Skylar a smoke and shrugged when she declined.

"No names," he said flatly as he struck a match against a cinder-block wall.

"Okay. I just want to know if you know that Svetlana is dead."

He exhaled a lungful of smoke that the wind snatched away at once and swore. "The bastard Banderas killed her," he said.

"I think so, but that's not how it was made to look. It

was made to look as though Svetlana murdered a friend and committed suicide."

He narrowed his eyes. "Why do you come here to tell me this?"

"Because Svetlana mentioned you were friends. She asked me to help her find Malina. I've hit a brick wall, but Svetlana told me Malina has a friend who works here. I can't remember her name."

"You mean Katerina," he said.

"That's right. Do you know when she'll be working? I'd like to ask her a few questions."

"She has a short shift from six to ten tonight." He stared at her a second from beneath heavy lids before adding, "If you want to speak with her you should do it somewhere else besides here."

"Do you know where she lives?"

"I gave her a ride once during a big snowstorm. She lives behind an old house about three blocks down."

"Did you ever talk to her about Malina and the man who befriended her?"

"You are talking about Ian Banderas again," he said, his voice growing very soft. "Lately, Katerina has caught his attention." He tossed the cigarette on the ground and stepped on it, twisting his shoe as he stood. "Listen. I need this job. I have children to support. I will not get in the middle of *anything*. You understand?"

"Yes," she told him, but he was already walking away.

Skylar took off again, this time down the street where the rejuvenation efforts quickly petered out to be replaced by rows of cookie-cutter houses. It seemed impossible she would be able to pick the right house out of so many, but there was one larger place that still claimed a yard of its own; the rest of the lots looked subdivided. And sure enough, when she looked, she could see a small detached building at the end of a narrow path through an untended garden.

Once again, she missed Cole's presence with an intensity that scorched her, but she pushed it aside and made her way down the path, anxious to speak with Katerina and learn something concrete that had nothing to do with Cole and that she could present to her uncle.

No one answered the door at the small cottage, although calling it a cottage was something of a stretch. Skylar tried looking in the window to the left of the door, but the drapes were pulled. Still, she had the feeling it was occupied, and she stepped off the tiny porch with the weird feeling someone was watching her.

She turned around and scanned the garden and saw nothing except dormant plants and dead weeds. To the side, she spied a spur of the path that led around to the back of the cottage, and she decided to follow that.

The back door was closed, but the window was undraped and Skylar looked inside. Her gaze traveled past the tiny kitchen and through the door that led to a bedroom. She could see the edge of a bed that caught afternoon shadows. One of them suddenly moved....

"Katerina?" she called, rapping on the door. "Please, I need to talk to you."

The shadow grew very still.

"I'm a friend of Svetlana's," she said, knocking again. "I know you're here. Please let me in."

It occurred to her that perhaps the shadow didn't belong to Katerina, and adrenaline surged through her body at the thought someone might be in there with the girl. Someone like Ian Banderas, perhaps. She tried the knob and the door opened. Swallowing what felt like a brick, she stepped inside.

"Stop right there," a voice said, and a frightened-looking young girl appeared in the doorway. About the same size as Skylar, she sported shaggy black hair, pale skin and dark-rimmed blue eyes.

There was nothing threatening about her except for the butcher knife clutched in one white-knuckled hand. "Who are you?" she snapped. "How did you get in here?"

"The door wasn't locked," Skylar said. She held her hands slightly aloft and did her best not to look confrontational. The girl's demeanor reminded her of Svetlana the night she'd clobbered Cole. Even mild-mannered people, when frightened enough, were capable of random acts of violence.

"Not locked?" She moved quickly toward Skylar who stepped out of her way. "The damn thing is broken again," she said as she twisted the brass knob and slammed the door. "Who are you? What do you know about Svetlana?"

"Are you Katerina, Malina's friend?" Looking slightly less terrified, the girl nodded and Skylar continued. "Her mother asked me to help her find out what happened to Malina." Skylar took a deep breath and imparted the news of Svetlana's death.

Katerina regarded Skylar with those strange icy eyes, made more pronounced by the black liner and the black hair that obscured half her face. The color couldn't be natural—it was way too dark for such light skin. "I'm sorry for her," she said, and walking past Skylar, she headed back to the bedroom.

Skylar followed, stopping at the door, her heart racing. A half-packed suitcase sat on the bed, drawers were pulled open and the closet door stood ajar.

"Where are you going?" Skylar asked.

Katerina looked over her shoulder. "Away."

"Like Malina did?"

"Who *are* you?" Katerina repeated, turning to sit down

beside her suitcase, the dark smudges under her eyes more pronounced in this light.

"My name is Skylar. I'm just trying to figure out what's going on. Are you leaving with Ian Banderas?"

"No!"

"The dishwasher at Pushki's said—"

"Sergi doesn't know anything. He doesn't want to know."

"What doesn't he want to know?"

"What Banderas is doing."

Skylar crossed the floor and sat down on the other side of the suitcase. "Tell me what's going on, please."

Now tears filled the dark-rimmed eyes. "I made a plan. I would go along with Ian and see where it took me so I could find Malina. Svetlana was supposed to watch out for me. But she disappeared a day ago, and now you tell me she's dead."

"Do you think Banderas is on to you, as well?"

"No. He thinks I'm leaving Kanistan tonight. He told me some big story about how I would have a brand-new start in America. He even gave me a little money and bought me this new suitcase. I'm supposed to meet Dasha tonight after work."

"Who's Dasha?"

"Ian says she is an embassy representative, and she will accompany us to America. I've never met her."

"Us? What do you mean?" Skylar asked.

"Me and a few other girls from other towns."

"So this, this ring of sorts, is not just here in Traterg."

"No."

"And they don't actually force anyone to go?"

Katerina looked down at her hands.

"What is it?"

"Malina told me she had changed her mind, and she

was going to tell Ian and Dasha she didn't want to leave. I did not tell this to Svetlana because I thought it would make things harder for her. Malina left to talk to them, but she never returned. I don't think she got out of Kanistan alive. But I couldn't take that hope away from Svetlana, could I?"

"No," Skylar said softly.

"I think they use restaurants to find girls who have run away or lied about themselves. Malina was different. She had her mom, not that she would ever admit as much. We both had to pretend to be eighteen and I was trying to disappear, so we didn't talk about family with anyone."

Skylar's thoughts momentarily skipped back to Chiaro and Aneta's family and the missing Zina who had also worked at a café. Apparently Banderas hadn't known Malina had a concerned mother until after the fact.

"Anyway, Dasha says I will have a new passport and documents and that I will work for an American family until I pay them back the money they spent for things like room and board, airfare and clothes," Katerina continued. "But I don't think you can ever work off the debt because it just keeps growing. Malina believed them at first. Then they gave her little pills to take—they said so she would not get airsick. Only they looked like some her mother got for pain when she broke her leg a year ago. Ian gave me those pills last night." She reached in her pocket and took out a small bottle with three pills in it. "Malina said all these do is make you like a zombie. I think that's when she decided not to go with them."

"I see," Skylar said as Katerina tossed the bottle on the bed.

"And I do not like the way they stress how nice I must be to everyone in my new American home," she added.

"How I must jump when they say to jump, especially the man. Do you know what I mean?"

"Yes," Skylar said, looking around the modest room. This poor kid had obviously had a hard time of it, and Skylar was glad she was heading back to wherever she called home. She noticed clothes and toiletries still scattered all over the place and added, "Can I help you pack the rest of your things?"

"I can't take anything else. My suitcase is full. Please, I have to go now."

"Just one more thing," Skylar pleaded. "This is important. Have you ever heard of a man named Luca Futura?"

"Yes."

"Have you met him?"

"No. Ian said his name several times."

"In what capacity? Is he involved with this situation?"

"I think so," she said. "But I'm not sure."

Skylar swallowed her heart as she took out her phone. "I'm going to call a cab that will take you any direction you want for fifty miles. Will that work?"

"I can't afford—"

"Don't worry. I'll pay for it."

"Then a ride across town to the train station would be great."

"Okay. But while we're walking to the street, you have to tell me exactly what the plan was for tonight. Okay?"

"Okay, okay," she said, shrugging on a coat and grabbing her suitcase. "Just hurry."

COLE RAN OUT OF THE AIRPORT to the welcome sight of a line of cabs all awaiting fares. He ducked into the closest one and yelled, "Go!" Apparently language barriers didn't exist when the voice delivering the message was urgent enough. The driver took off, and Cole sat back in the seat, still clutching his briefcase.

He'd never intended on taking that plane—not tonight anyway—but he also hadn't planned on an attack so quickly. Maybe the fact it came so fast explained the amateur efforts of his assailants—not that amateurs didn't occasionally get the job done.

He needed to get to a phone. Without Skylar to help translate, he was stuck in the water because the only option left now was to find a way to blend in. He took a couple of deep breaths to steady his nerves.

As the cab rolled into the city, Cole spotted a row of shabby hotels, and a few blocks later, he asked the driver to stop. Again, his message seemed to get through because within moments he had paid the tab and was walking back down the block, nervously looking around for signs he'd been followed. He couldn't see anybody, but that didn't mean they weren't there. He checked in using cash and went up to his room where he used a credit card to place a call to Slovo.

She answered on the third ring. "Irina Churo," she said.

"It's Cole Bennett," he told her. "I need help. Tonight. Can you drive down here?"

Her voice lowered. "No, I'm sorry. I just can't. I'm covering for a guy whose wife just went into labor. I can meet you tomorrow. Will that work?"

"I guess it has to," he said. He gave her the name of the hotel he had checked into and a general sketch of his plan. After he hung up, he placed another call, this one to Skylar. As it rang and rang, he pictured her staring at the strange number on the screen, sensing it was him while digital strains of *Raiders of the Lost Ark* filled the air.

She didn't answer, and he decided not to leave a message.

Then he opened his briefcase. It was a miracle he'd managed to keep it during the attack. Tonight he would reconnoiter; tomorrow, Irina and he would do the rest.

THE IDEA CAME TO SKYLAR when, without anywhere else to go, she'd decided to hang out at Katerina's place in case Ian or Dasha showed up and she could confront them. She assumed her status as her uncle's niece would protect her from their violence, but the truth was she was so upset by Svetlana's death and the audacity of the people who murdered her and her friend that she almost welcomed a confrontation.

As for the bombshell that Katerina dropped? That she couldn't bear to believe—not only for her aunt's sake but for Cole's. Had she been so blinded by loyalty to her family that she'd jeopardized the man she loved, that she refused to stand beside him when he needed her most?

Katerina had left a box of black hair dye on the drain board, and as soon as Skylar saw it, the wheels began to spin. They were about the same size and bone structure. Katerina's makeup and haircut were so distinctive they defined her, and they were both things Skylar could imitate. Surely fate had stepped in....

She had to know how deep her uncle was in this mess, and that was going to take a little risk.

An hour later, her hair was as black as midnight and with the help of kitchen shears just about as ragged as Katerina's, falling forward over half her face. She found a ratty pair of jeans Katerina had probably left behind because they were so big they fell off if not belted and a T-shirt cast aside in the closet along with an apron embroidered with Pushki's. Even the girl's shoes fit tolerably well although they each had a hole in the sole. All that was left to do was make up her eyes with the almost-empty container of discarded eyeliner she found and lower the pitch of her voice.

With any luck, the staff and patrons would see exactly what they expected to see as Skylar assumed Katerina's identity and assured whoever—if anyone—was watching her that everything was fine and going according to plan. And since she'd worked a semester during college waiting tables, there was a good chance she could make this work.

Skylar walked back to the café without a coat as hers was red and highly visible and nothing like the clothes Katerina wore. The cook looked up as she entered the kitchen. "'Bout time you showed up."

She shrugged and didn't respond, pleased that so far she'd been taken at face value. An older waitress told her to get out on the floor, that she had tables ten through twenty and things were getting busy. She found a chart on the wall and paused in front of it long enough to get an idea of where her tables were located.

The café had been smoky in the middle of the day, but now it was worse. Groups of people looking as though they were fresh from work sat at round tables drinking everything from coffee to wine, and it wasn't long before she was taking orders and turning in tickets by watching how the other waitresses did it. Her main fear was that a cook would notice her handwriting wasn't the same as Katerina's, or perhaps that she wasn't using the right codes, but she kept at it, looking at other tickets whenever she could.

It was a noisy, boisterous crowd who all called her by name and asked her questions that she responded to with flippant answers and vague waves of the hand. Katerina had told her that Dasha would come to Katerina's house after the café closed at ten o'clock but that she suspected the woman might come earlier to the café just to make sure things were on schedule. Dasha would give Katerina a ride to the airport, a new American passport and documentation, then she would fly with Katerina and an undisclosed number of other girls to the United States. Entry into the country would be mere formality, Katerina was assured, because of Dasha's diplomatic connection. And it was important that Katerina take all three of the small white pills she'd been given as soon as she got home.

Skylar had called the airport and found that there was a commercial flight leaving for New York that night. And then she'd stared at her phone and tried to decide if she should tell anyone what she was up to. With Cole out of the picture, the only person she could confide in was her uncle. Not right now, no thanks.

She'd had several hours to think about what Cole had told her that morning and review his actions of the past few days, and now she was able to consider the possibility that some of what had happened between them might be real. Every look, every caress, every whispered word couldn't have been a lie. Or was that wishful thinking?

As far as how she would provide proof damning enough to make her uncle wake up and smell the coffee—well, that she wasn't sure about. It was her first time as a spy, and she was winging it.

"Katerina!" the waitress named Rosa said. "Your order is waiting. Wake up, girl!"

"Oh, sorry," Skylar said, scooping up a platter of sausage and potatoes.

"It's okay," Rosa said. "You look a little different tonight. Maybe a little preoccupied?"

"Maybe," Skylar said.

"You have another admirer," Rosa added.

"Another?"

"Besides the cute blond guy that started coming onto

you after Malina left him high and dry. There's a new one, over near the kitchen. He's been staring at you."

Skylar hadn't noticed anyone staring at her, which was a little disconcerting. She'd been so busy trying to be Katerina that she hadn't been wary enough. This time when she delivered her order, she peered into the shadowed edges of the room and saw a dark-haired man with a beard and thick glasses nursing coffee and smoking brown cigarettes. He held a book and didn't seem to be watching anyone. Maybe Rosa was imagining things.

By then, the after-dinner crowd began to show up, including a lone woman who looked vaguely familiar to Skylar. She was relieved when the woman chose another waitress's table, afraid they may have met at some time.

Who was she? Blunt-cut black hair, ruby-red lips, pretty…she could hear Cole saying something: pretty in a *"she-eats-minions-for-lunch way."* That's what he'd said about this woman when she came into the hotel dining room with Ian Banderas. Was this Dasha?

Skylar got very busy for a while, but she tried to keep an eye on the two people of interest. The woman left after eating a cup of soup. Skylar didn't notice when the man left; he was just suddenly gone.

It was after ten by the time Skylar tallied her tickets, collected her tips and made her way out the door. Before checking in at the café, she'd replaced the three little sleeping pills with aspirin and left them on the counter of Katerina's home. Since there was no way to lock the door, she'd also straightened things up so that if someone checked they wouldn't immediately suspect the real Katerina had vacated the premises.

The sidewalks were slippery with icy rain. Without a coat, the cold encouraged her to hurry. Her phone was in her pocket, and she kept her hand over it because twice that evening it had almost fallen out. She'd actually snapped a quick shot of the woman in the café already, but it was dark and grainy. Besides, the person she really wanted to capture was Ian Banderas.

The garden path at night resembled something out of a horror movie with waving black limbs and blowing leaves. She let herself into Katerina's old house with a sigh of relief.

That sigh was premature as the lights suddenly clicked on, and she found the woman from the restaurant standing by the counter, a clothes bag in her hands.

"Sorry to startle you," she said, her voice as crisp as her haircut. She wore a blue wool jacket with a complicated insignia on the lapel over a long black skirt. It was the emblem of the Kanistan embassy; Skylar had seen it before when she'd visited with her uncle. So that's how they moved people around. Heeled boots made her tower over Skylar. "My name is Dasha, your embassy connection. Ian told you I would come, didn't he?"

"Yes, ma'am," she said, hoping to appear demure.

"Have you taken your pills yet?"

"No, ma'am."

"Take them now," Dasha said. "Ian will be here in a few minutes."

Ian was coming! This was great news. She could get this on the camera, maybe even hit the movie mode so it recorded voices. She took the small bottle from the counter and emptied the contents—three aspirin masquerading as barbiturates—into her hand, swallowing them with the aid of a glass of water Dasha handed her.

"And change into this," Dasha added, shoving the clothes bag at Skylar.

Skylar took the bag and saw immediately that it held the same outfit that Dasha wore. She retreated to the small bedroom and wondered how she would transfer her phone between clothes.

"Please, hurry," Dasha said, and it was clear she was going to stand at the door and watch. Skylar took the bag and retreated into the bathroom. The first thing she did was check to see if her wallet, which she'd hidden under a pile of dirty towels, was still there, sighing with relief when she found it was. She changed out of Katerina's old jeans and shirt quickly, stuffing them into the small trash can, donning the skirt and jacket. Neither article had pockets. With nowhere to conceal the phone, she stuck it in the trash can with her clothes. She would have to think of an excuse to use the bathroom again before she left.

"That's better," Dasha said when she returned and the critical cast of her gaze made Skylar glad she'd ditched her wallet and phone.

"Where is your new suitcase?" Dasha asked. "I don't see it here."

"I sold it," Skylar said.

"And the money Ian gave you to settle your obligations?"

"I spent it all," Skylar said.

Dasha shook her head. "I'll give you your passport when we get to the airport. From now on, you'll be Susan Williams from Seattle, Washington. Are you excited about your grand new adventure?"

"Yes," Skylar said.

"Good for you. Oh, and by the way, we did a little checking and discovered you have family you failed to mention. We know exactly where they live. You have a little sister, too, no? Rest assured, we will send them a note to explain your absence along with a little extra cash to help them along."

They'd found Katerina's family? Skylar started to rub

her eyes, remembered all the makeup and stopped herself. Was mentioning the sister some kind of veiled threat? Was this how they made sure the girls wouldn't get cold feet? Katerina had assumed they didn't know about her family, but obviously, they did.

"I know you switched the pills," Dasha said, a little of the sugary sweetness missing from her voice. "Why did you do that?"

"I, um, sold those, too."

"Enterprising little thing, aren't you? Well, never fear, I switched them back. We can't have you airsick."

Call it the power of suggestion, but with the knowledge that she'd taken the wrong pills Skylar became lightheaded. This couldn't happen; she needed to keep her wits. As she stepped away from Dasha, the room spun and she stumbled.

Dasha handed Skylar her red coat. "I found that in the bedroom. I'm surprised you didn't sell it, too. Put it over your uniform."

There was a quick knocking sound. As Dasha answered the door, Skylar put on her coat. Now she had a pocket. Ian Banderas slipped inside with a draft of cold air. This was what Skylar had been waiting for, but now that the moment to act was upon her, she couldn't. What's more, her head swam, and she looked longingly toward the bathroom that suddenly seemed a mile away.

"Help me get her out to the van," Dasha said.

"What's wrong with her?"

"The pills. She'll snap out of it."

"Where's her suitcase?"

"She sold it. We'll check one of my bags as hers so it won't look suspicious."

"Bathroom," Skylar managed to mutter, but it sounded garbled to her own ears and they ignored her. Banderas clutched her arm. "I have good news for you," he crooned into her ear. "Your friend Malina worked out so well the sponsoring family wants another helper. Won't it be nice to see her again?" He soothed her hair. "You're going to have a new life, sweetheart. You're going to be an American!"

Malina was alive!

Ian turned back to Dasha. "The family is paying extra for you to deliver her to their estate."

"What do I do with the other girls while I'm driving around with her?"

"Someone will meet you at the airport and take them to their next destination. Here," he continued, producing a paper and pencil. "Write a note and leave it on the table for her landlady. Put a few euros with it. Hurry up."

All Skylar could think about was the fact Malina wasn't dead. There was a chance to save her, a chance for Skylar to redeem herself, to make amends for getting the girl's mother killed.

"Did your men get Bennett?"

"We'll discuss that later," Ian said.

Get Bennett? Had they tried to hurt Cole? The elation of a moment before disappeared into the certainty of what they would do to Cole if they found him.

"You're getting careless, Ian," Dasha said, switching to English, probably so the girl they thought was Katerina wouldn't understand them. "Too many people know about you."

"I've cleaned up my share of dead ends," he replied.

"What do you mean by that?"

"I mean you had one simple job to do in Slovo, and you botched it."

"The girl is Futura's niece," Dasha said.

"Yes, and she is getting close to discovering I killed

Aneta. That bitch actually threatened me. Anyway, because of Futura's niece, we're going to have to cut this venture short or figure out a way to eliminate her." He looked at Skylar, who didn't have to work too hard to appear spaced out. Hearing her uncle's name on top of Malina's and Cole's left her reeling, let alone their plans for her.

Dasha was undeterred. "When he finds out the messy way you went about taking care of this latest little problem and her friend, he's going to come unglued."

"What's he going to do? I own him, and he owns the police. Everything is fine. Are you done with that note yet?"

"Yes."

"Come on, Katerina," Ian said to Skylar. "Let's get to the airport." Dasha took the other arm, and they left the little house together, not bothering to turn off the lights or close the door. The walk through the garden seemed interminable. They approached a van, and the next thing she knew, Skylar was being helped into the back. The door slid shut, and the van took off.

Under the cover of darkness, tears filled Skylar's eyes as she thought of Svetlana and all the others—and most of all, Cole. She'd pushed him away when she should have found a way to work with him. And now she might never have the chance to feel his arms around her again.

Chapter Sixteen

Cole blended into the trees as three people left the house he'd trailed Katerina to a short while before.

His idea had been to identify Katerina at Pushki's then find out where she lived so he and Irina could approach her the next day. The addition of phony facial hair, knit cap and thick glasses gave him a sense of anonymity, and things had gone according to plan. Once he'd trailed her through the garden, however, he'd seen her lights go on and heard another woman's voice so he'd crouched under a window and listened. Soon after that, Ian Danderas arrived. The walls were so thin the voices were clear, but he couldn't understand a blasted word until they switched to English and argued about who was the more efficient thug.

And then that flash of red he'd seen when the door had opened just now. If that coat wasn't Skylar's, it was its double. Katerina hadn't been wearing it when she left the restaurant, so how did it end up on her back now?

Maybe Skylar had come to talk to her and left it here or had it taken from her....

"Skylar?" he murmured, ducking into the house, pausing at the bedroom doorway, half expecting to find her lifeless body, sighing with relief when he found nothing. He walked back into the living space that combined the kitchen and a couple of chairs at a small table, uncertain what to make of this. He noticed the note on the table but couldn't read it.

Maybe there were other coats like Skylar's, but hadn't she told him the first night they had dinner that she made hers and it was a one of a kind? Still, a red coat was a red coat, right?

A very soft vibrating noise suddenly caught his attention, and he turned in a wide circle to see where it came from. The place looked all but abandoned. He opened a few drawers, but they were mostly empty. Eventually he found himself heading toward the bedroom where, upon a closer look, he found a few pieces of clothes he recognized as Skylar's stacked on the top shelf of the closet. His heart sank.

The noise started again, and this time it was closer and more distinct. He walked into the tiny bathroom and picked up the small garbage can, lifting old clothes and finding a cell phone set on vibrating mode. With the sweep of a finger, he turned on the screen. The ID showed the call was from Skylar's aunt. Taking care not to answer the call, he checked the information screen. Yep, it was Skylar's. If her phone and clothes had been abandoned in this shabby little hole in the wall, it meant something had happened to her. The girl wearing her coat was his one and only lead.

He racked his brain, trying to remember if he'd understood anything of the conversation he'd overheard. He had recognized Skylar's and Futura's names and even his own. And he'd heard reference to the airport.

Of course. The airport.

The phone stopped vibrating. He slipped it in his pocket, then left, running up the path and back to the café area where he could hail a cab. His knee throbbed with the exertion, but he ignored the pain. He had to get to the airport—now.

IT WAS IMPOSSIBLE NOT TO notice the extra security, thanks, no doubt, to the dead body in the bathroom. Cole did his best to blend in, extra glad of the disguise.

If Banderas and company were going to America and they weren't taking a private jet, then they had to be on the flight Cole was already checked in to. He took a circuitous route to his terminal, ditched the beard and the glasses and kept the mustache.

As casually as he could, he inspected the other passengers waiting in the enclosed area. He found no sign of Katerina and began to panic. Maybe he'd misunderstood the word for airport or maybe there was a private strip.

Boarding for first-class passengers began but he held back, his patience eventually rewarded when he spied the striking brunette in an official-looking jacket coming toward him. She was surrounded by four girls, one of them Katerina. They all appeared to be a little scared, a little excited and a little drugged, and they, too, all wore the same jacket and even the same long black skirt as though part of a group. He had to find a way to separate Katerina from the rest and ask her about Skylar.

Nearby, he noticed Banderas standing with arms crossed, surveying the area from a distance. It didn't appear he was boarding. While firearms weren't allowed in the airport, there wasn't a doubt in his mind Banderas could get around that rule easily, and Cole would be willing to bet his own face was at least known to the man.

To make things worse, the guy from the incident in the bathroom was prowling the area. It was only a matter of time before they spotted him. Add all the airport security they could summon that he could not and the whole thing became daunting.

What was he supposed to do? If he used his ticket, these two would be informed, and he'd be hauled off the plane and that would be the end of him. If he approached the woman holding Katerina, he'd be nabbed as well. He pulled his hat down and hunkered in a seat, staring at Katerina, making and discarding plans.

And that's when her gaze met his, and he felt a jolt of recognition that shook him to his soul. His pulse raced; his mouth went dry. How could he not have realized it was Skylar under all that makeup? Her nose, her lips, her alpine-blue eyes? His heart lodged in his throat.

He expected her to break away and run to him or at least plead silently for help. His body tensed as he plotted a way to put himself between her and Banderas. But Skylar looked away at once. Was it because she hated him? No, that wasn't it. He'd seen the same flash of longing on her face that he felt in his heart. For reasons of her own, she didn't want him to interfere.

She boarded the plane with the others, and Cole managed a shaky breath. Now all he had to do was figure out a way to board without Banderas and his crony getting wind of it, but amazingly enough, that problem seemed to melt away. The two men sauntered off as though it never occurred to them Cole would be at the airport.

Last chance boarding was announced. Cole checked in at the desk and ran to make the plane. His goal was finally obvious to him, his mission defined with crystal clarity: save Skylar at any cost.

SKYLAR KEPT HER MOUTH SHUT as she'd been instructed. Her mind, however, was screaming at the top of its lungs: she'd seen Cole!

He'd changed a little in the hours they'd spent apart. He'd acquired a hat and a plaid jacket and a mustache, but it was him, in the flesh. It had taken every ounce of self-control she possessed not to reach out to him.

She wasn't sure how involved her uncle was in this horrible ring Dasha and Ian were running. She wanted him to be an innocent victim, but she kept going over what Cole had told her of the past and the way her uncle had spoken when she questioned him. He'd been hiding something, she knew that; maybe she'd always known that.

As much as she wanted to blame Ian Banderas for everything, Ian had been a small boy thirty years before. He couldn't have been responsible for destroying Cole's family.

She wanted a chance to tell Cole she should have given him the opportunity to explain things better, she should have tried to keep an open mind and not been blinded by family loyalty and her own pride. Lovers worked things out and they helped each other. Despite the way he'd lied to her, she was finally able to admit that the depth of their feelings for each other was real. No man could fake what she'd seen in Cole's eyes a few moments before, and no woman could deny what Skylar felt in her heart.

But he mustn't try to help her until she found Malina, and she had no way of telling him that. Her gut said he was on this plane, but she could hardly parade around and look for him. She'd been told to keep quiet, answer only to the name Susan, and stay in her seat. She had the uneasy feeling there would be additional drugs: it was a ten-hour flight. But this time, come hell or high water, she wouldn't take them. She fell asleep with that thought.

THANKS TO TIME CHANGES, it was still the middle of the night when they landed. When going through customs, Cole strained to keep an eye out for Skylar. He cleared before her group and went into the waiting area where he took up a spot around a corner.

For an instant, he toyed around with alerting the authorities but abandoned it. Who would believe him? Besides, he had to trust Skylar's motives for advancing this charade. There must be something important at stake, and he didn't know what it was.

The group finally emerged from customs. Cole couldn't take his gaze off Skylar. She looked pale and tired, but the sparkle was back in her eyes, and he could tell she was pretending to be as sleepy as everyone else. She kept with the group, but as she passed him, she glanced up, and Cole swore she mouthed the word, "Follow."

After they had gone on by, Cole did just that. They went through baggage claims together and moved in a group outside where the sun was just beginning to rise.

The embassy woman began talking to the girls. Cole made a big deal out of looking like a perturbed commuter awaiting a ride. Eventually, a harried-looking man arrived. The embassy woman gave him a manila envelope bulging with papers and sent him back inside with the other girls as if to catch a new flight.

The woman hailed a cab, and Cole saw Skylar and her get into the cab. He got in the one right behind it and tapped the driver on the shoulder. "Stay with the cab in front, but don't be too obvious," he said.

The driver got into the spirit of the thing and stayed a good distance behind. The ground was covered with snow, the tree limbs bare and black as they drove into the countryside. The burgeoning light lay low and heavy in the leaden sky.

It took well over two hours before the cab turned into the private estate of a huge house in a valley outside the city. The gates closed behind it. Cole got out of the cab and stood for a moment considering his options as his breath condensed around his face.

Prudence said to guard the gate and wait for what

comes next. A normal guy might enlist the aid of the cops. But Cole, in his heart of hearts, was still a soldier, and sometimes a soldier had to take calculated risks.

He got back in the cab. "Drive me to the nearest town," he said. "And hurry."

THE WAY DONALD KESTER looked Skylar up and down gave her the creeps. His patrician face was cold, his gaze calculating. He looked like he ate kittens for breakfast.

His wife, Esther, wasn't much better. Prim, thin and with a beaked nose, she and her husband made a dandy pair. "This girl is a ragamuffin," Esther said in clipped English.

"Mrs. Kester, please. She will clean up very pretty," Dasha responded.

"Look at her hair. It appears to have been cut with a lawn mower."

The man blinked as he raked Skylar's body with his eyes. "We'll take her. You can have the other one back."

"Back?" Dasha said. "What do you mean, back? I thought you wanted two of them. I can't take Malina back."

"We no longer wish to support her," the man said. "She cries all the time."

"Is she good with your children?" Dasha asked.

Esther tilted her long head. "Shall we just be blunt? Our children are away at a boarding school most of the time. The girl is here to do my bidding and provide… entertainment…for my husband. She is slow with the housework and uncooperative in the bedroom." She looked at Skylar again and sighed. "At least this one seems to have a little fire in her eyes."

Dasha, assuming Skylar couldn't understand a word of this, smiled as though to reassure her everything was fine.

You unmitigated bitch were the words that sailed through Skylar's mind as she returned the smile. "I'll have to contact my partner," Dasha continued. "I can't possibly take her today. A new…situation…will have to be found. Tomorrow morning would be the soonest."

"That's acceptable," the man interrupted. "Now, tell the girl to come with me. I'll be right back to complete this transaction."

Dasha switched languages and directed Skylar to follow the man. As he led her across the foyer, Skylar was afraid he'd try to grab her and she'd have to let him have it. She couldn't let that happen; she had to find Malina. Then it was just a matter of applying a little Yankee ingenuity. Breaking a window, perhaps, appealing to the other servants, such as the guy who had ushered them in a short while ago. If Malina didn't speak English, how could she plead her case with Americans? But Skylar was here now. Things would change—and soon, too.

"You're a pretty little thing," Mr. Kester said, turning to leer at her. He had to know she supposedly couldn't understand him, but he continued anyway. "You'll have to share a room tonight with that wretch, but she'll be gone tomorrow and then you and I can get acquainted."

Over my dead body, Skylar whispered in her head.

He took her up a flight of stairs, then unlocked a door at the end of a hallway. With a none too gentle push, he sent her inside the room. "Welcome to your new home, Katerina," he said as he shut the door and relocked it. Skylar listened to his retreating footsteps.

"Katerina?"

Skylar turned. A young version of Svetlana looked up at her from a chair across the room.

"You're not Katerina," the girl said, her voice falling.

"You must be Malina. I'll explain everything."

"Did you bring help?" Malina asked.

"I'm not positive," Skylar said, "but either which way, I'll get you out of here and soon, too."

"Are you nuts? Take a look around you. There are no windows, and the only door is locked. I'm never allowed around the others without supervision. You've just become a prisoner, like me."

HE WASN'T POSITIVE SHE was still in the house, but he had to proceed under the assumption she was. The day had gone on forever, but three hours before a lone woman had driven away in an old car so he assumed some of the help had left. Then about an hour ago, he'd seen the upstairs lights flicker off. The family should be asleep by now. Time to go to work.

"Are you sure you just want me to hang around out here?" Tyler asked.

"Yeah," Cole replied. He'd called both his brothers from town. John was caught in the Midwest's worst snowstorm of the century, but Tyler had actually been in New York, with his wife, Juliet, where they'd been enjoying a small vacation before the upcoming birth of their first child. He'd dropped everything and driven up here, arriving a little while ago. He was as big as Cole, about two years older, a good-looking guy partial to vests and jeans and boots as befitted a cattle rancher. Cole had spent the past thirty minutes bringing him up to speed with what was going on here and in Kanistan.

"I don't like you going in there alone," Tyler insisted.

"I need you out here," Cole said. "If things go wrong, you'll need to make them right. And if they go right, I need you to cover my ass. If you don't hear from me in an hour, then I guess it's time to call in reinforcements and let the dust settle where it may."

"You've got an hour," Tyler said.

"And if they do go wrong," Cole added, "tell Skylar I love her and I'm sorry for everything."

Tyler walked back to his truck, calling over his shoulder, "You can tell her that yourself."

That was the plan, but everyone knew things didn't always go according to plan.

Chapter Seventeen

Cole's foray into the nearest sporting-goods store had resulted in snow camouflage gear, a spotting scope, good boots, rope, a grappling hook, a lethal-looking hunting knife and a few other supplies that he wore strapped to his body. He'd spent the afternoon preparing his gear and scouting the layout.

The grappling hook sailed over a spot in the wall where the mortar between the rocks had crumpled, making it a good place to scramble up the face. He dropped down inside the property for the second time that day, taking the major impact on his right leg to spare his left knee, but the pain still jolted him as he hit. For a second, he lay in the snow, chiding the sorry mess he'd become, then got back to business.

He knew from a daylight excursion he'd made a few hours earlier that the power lines to the alarm system ran to a locked outbuilding near the fence, and he made his way for that now, the limp more pronounced than before. He'd asked around in town, and it appeared that during the winter the only residents were the couple who owned the place and a few servants. No one seemed to know anything about young, foreign-speaking women.

He couldn't think about Skylar. Not yet. He had no idea

what she was up to, and if he let it, doubt crept in that she was even still here.

The lock on the outbuilding was no match for bolt cutters. Once inside, he kept the lights off, using a small, bright beam to find the control box. It was an old unit, hardly state-of-the-art, one Cole had experience with from military duty. It wasn't long before the alarm was disabled, and he was on his way to what he knew from watching the house through his scope for most of the day was the kitchen.

The lock on that door gave in easily, and he entered silently. He could hear a TV on nearby and followed the sound to a small room beyond the kitchen where a man of about fifty sat in a chair facing the TV. Four empty cans of beer beside him and an open one in his hand helped explain the snoring.

Cole shook the guy's shoulder making sure the first thing he saw when he opened his eyes was the blade of the hunting knife. "Not a peep," Cole said.

The guy shook his head vehemently as he lost control of the open can and beer spilled in his lap.

"I'm not here to hurt anyone or steal anything. Who are you?"

It appeared the guy had to work saliva into his mouth before he could mumble, "I'm just the handyman. What do you want?"

"I'm looking for the foreign girl."

"She doesn't speak any English. They keep her locked in her room upstairs when she isn't working."

She was here! "Which room?"

"End of the hall."

"Where's the cook's room?"

"She doesn't stay here at night."

She must have been the woman he saw driving away a

couple hours ago. Cole took out a roll of duct tape. "I'm going to make sure you don't raise the household."

"Just don't hurt me."

A few minutes later, Cole left the gagged man taped to the sofa and started toward the stairs. The hall split in two directions at the top and he paused. Something about the paintings on the wall and the fresh flowers on a table in the left passage suggested it led to the owners' suite so he turned left. He had no intention of alerting anyone else he was in the house. All he wanted was Skylar.

The lock at the end of the hall was a little harder to pick than he'd anticipated, and doing it while holding the flashlight between his teeth made it tedious work. He was worried about the time. No matter what these people were guilty of when it came to importing and mistreating illegal workers, he'd broken into their home and threatened their servant with a knife. If Tyler called the police, guess who would be going to jail first?

The lock finally clicked, and it sounded to Cole's sensitive ears like a bomb exploding. He eased the door open as an innocent scream of surprise could awaken the wrong people just as a warning could. "Skylar?" he said into the dark, hesitant to flash the light that it would blind and frighten her.

"Cole?"

He risked the light then and took in the room with one glance. It looked like a windowless cell of some kind with twin beds, each occupied, one by a sleeping girl in the process of waking up and one by Skylar, who sat atop the bedspread, fully clothed, holding a sharpened pencil as though it were a weapon. She dropped the pencil and rose to her feet, her gaze fastened to his. He approached her in a daze.

"Are you all right?" he whispered, touching her chopped black hair and then her cheek.

"I am now," she said, her voice shaking.

"I'm sorry," he said. "I should never have lied to you. I never expected I would fall in love with you—"

She stilled him with her lips, as soft as velvet, her fragrance as sensual and memorable as always. "I'm sorry, too," she said. "I should have worked with you. You almost got killed because of me."

He closed his eyes for a second, and that's when he noticed the girl in the other bed was talking a mile a minute, frantic, her voice too loud. He pulled away from Skylar. "Who is she?"

"Svetlana's daughter, Malina," Skylar said.

"Tell her to keep it down. I'll stand guard while she finds a coat and shoes. We only have four and a half minutes to get back to Tyler."

"Hold it right there," a male voice said from behind him.

Cole could have kicked himself. He'd made the biggest rookie mistake in the book. He'd neglected to watch his back.

HOPE TURNED TO DREAD in the blink of an eye as Skylar caught sight of Donald Kester with a gun.

Cole had turned by then—he stood between Kester and her and Malina. Cole was hard to overlook in his white-and-gray camouflage with a dozen things strapped to his waist, shoulders broad, body big and strong. And he'd said he'd loved her.

"Hand me the knife," Kester said.

Cole shook his head. "No."

"Who the hell are you breaking into my house in the middle of the night, threatening my domestic help?"

"Is that what you're calling this?" Cole said, his voice relaxed. "Interesting choice. I'd call it slavery, or maybe even something worse."

"You don't know what you're talking about," Kester scoffed. "We give these girls a chance for a good life."

"Yeah. Right. Why are they locked in this room? Why have you bordered up their windows?"

Kester jostled the gun. "For their own safety. Come with me."

"If I don't, what are you going to do?" Cole said easily. "Call the police? Go ahead. Call them. Get your wife up. Let's get this all out in the open."

"My wife is out like a light," Kester said. "Whatever happens next, it'll be my word against yours, and I dare say my word is worth more."

"You're forgetting about me," Skylar said, pleased to see the shock in Kester's eyes as she spoke English. "And I can translate for Malina Dacho." She'd spent half the day telling Malina about what had happened to her mother, consoling her and promising if Malina wanted to live in the States, Skylar would be a legitimate sponsor on the West Coast. "I just want you to know you are indirectly responsible for the death of Malina's mother and several other people. Your greedy appetites have helped wreck a lot of lives."

"So say you. This girl was introduced to us as Linda Armstrong from Detroit. First-generation American. Raised in a family where she was not allowed to speak English. I have her passport and papers to prove it. Just as I have papers claiming you are Susan Williams. Obviously I'm being scammed."

"Nice try," Skylar said, "but you're forgetting I understood every word you spoke to Dasha earlier today."

"No one would blame me for shooting an intruder,"

Kester said, waving his gun, turning his attention back to Cole. His nerves were beginning to show. "If someone else gets killed in the process, it's not my fault."

All of a sudden the partially closed door banged open and another man appeared. With a thump on the top of his head from the butt of the newcomer's big silver gun, Kester keeled over into Cole's arms.

"I got tired of waiting," the man said. He looked at Skylar and added, "My name is Tyler Hunt, ma'am, and I'm Cole's older brother. Well, one of them, anyway. You must be Skylar. I'm very happy to meet you."

"Not half as happy as I am to meet you," Skylar responded truthfully.

Tyler grinned as he tousled Cole's hair. "You know, little brother, I knew the day I found out about the past that my life was going to change, but I never guessed just how much."

Cole laughed.

THEY SLEPT ALL THE WAY back to Kanistan, wrapped in each other's arms. Skylar had had to use Katerina's fake passport, as she didn't have her real one with her, and time was of the essence. They didn't want to take a chance that Banderas or anyone else would find out what had happened at the Kester house and destroy the papers that would reveal how many girls were missing and where they could be found. For that reason they'd left Tyler in charge of watching Malina and the Kesters and greeting Dasha when she came to collect Malina. They'd have to figure out the police angle of everything later.

"How are we going to find Banderas?" he asked Skylar as they got into the rental car. He glanced over at her as he spoke and experienced a little quiver. He couldn't believe they'd found their way back to one another, and if this Skylar didn't quite look like the one he'd made love to, that was okay. She was beautiful no matter what, but he was glad the heavy makeup was gone and he could really see her face.

"I think he'll probably find us."

"Do you have a plan? Let's remember this man and his cohort have tried to kill both of us and succeeded with at least three others."

"I haven't forgotten," Skylar said, her gaze fastened straight ahead. "But first things first."

He didn't have to ask what she meant. He knew she had to do this thing her way, and for once, he didn't need to be in command; his job was to keep her alive.

THE HOUSE WAS VERY QUIET when the butler let them in the door. "Where is everyone?" Skylar asked, and it was a sign of the man's training that he didn't react to her radical new appearance. "Master is in his office," he said. "Madame is upstairs."

Her aunt's nurse came out of the kitchen bearing a tray. When she saw Skylar, she almost dropped it. "Is that you, Ms. Pope?" she asked.

"Yes. How is my aunt?"

"Doing better. She's had a couple of days without treatments, and she's getting stronger. She was worried about you, though. Didn't you get her call?"

"It's a long story," Skylar said.

The nurse seemed to notice Cole for the first time, which was pretty astounding in Skylar's book. While he was no longer wearing his camouflage gear, he was an imposing man in his quiet, substantial, don't-cross-me way, and when he was around, she had a hard time noticing anyone or anything else. The nurse hurried away, and the butler melted into the house. As they approached the office, Skylar spoke. "Let me talk to him alone for a moment."

"If I've learned anything in the past twenty-four hours it's that you and I work best when we're together."

She paused to look up at him. "I think you've changed a little," she said.

"Well, I am no longer a card-carrying loner," he responded as he leaned down and kissed her. "You can handle this any way you want, but let me be nearby."

She nodded and knocked on the door. A distracted voice called, "Come in, come in." They found her uncle standing with his back to the room, closing the safe that was hidden behind the wedding portrait.

"You're early," he said. "And this is the last—"

By this time, he'd turned and found Skylar and Cole standing inside the room. His eyebrows rose, probably because Skylar looked so different. "Oh," he said.

"You were expecting somebody else," Skylar said.

"Well, yes."

"Ian Banderas?"

"As a matter of fact…"

"And what's that in your hand, Uncle Luca?"

He looked down at the envelope he held but said nothing.

"That's why Banderas is in and out of here all the time, isn't it?" Skylar said. "I heard him tell someone you were powerless to stop him because he owned you. He's blackmailing you, isn't he?"

"Don't be absurd," he said, setting the envelope down on the desk. "What in the world have you done to yourself, and why is this man in my house?"

"I'm just making sure she's okay," Cole said.

"She hardly needs you to look after her."

"On the contrary, Mr. Futura. You've been so busy

covering up your past that you were willing to sacrifice her future."

"And you're talking in riddles."

"Am I? I take it Banderas is expected any minute. Shall we wait for him? He can help explain why Skylar looks the way she does and where she's been the past couple of days. I think you'll find his story quite compelling."

Skylar's uncle looked at her. "What is he talking about?"

"Ian Banderas and a member of your embassy, a woman named Dasha something, have been spiriting away young girls with false passports and identities to America, where they are good as sold to the highest bidder. I have repeatedly tried to get you to acknowledge that something was going on and you have refused. And I have the horrible feeling that you've known about it all along."

"Skylar, I've been patient. But really, this is tiresome and I am expecting Mr. Banderas on a private matter, so perhaps you and—"

"My name is not really Cole Bennett," Cole said, and in that moment Skylar remembered that this situation wasn't hers alone. It belonged to Cole and his brothers, as well. "My real name, the name you stole from me along with the lives of my parents, is Cole Oates. I believe we may have met before, say, when I was two."

"That's impossible," Luca said after an icy pause.

Cole moved farther into the room, but Skylar stayed back by the open door. His white-knuckled fists at his sides and the purposeful way he moved betrayed the emotions she knew ate at his heart. It was probably all he could do not to slam his fist into her uncle's face.

His voice was very soft when he spoke. "You killed my parents, you bastard, and then you covered it up by shipping their two small children off to America and as good as imprisoned the third."

"You are insane."

"Don't lie to me," Cole warned. "I know you did it. My brothers know you did it. None of us will rest until you've paid for what you've done. Charles and Mary Oates trusted you, and you betrayed them. You destroyed the Roman family in the bargain, and now you're about to destroy your own. All because you wouldn't take responsibility for impregnating Lenora Roman."

"What is going on?" Ian Banderas said as he entered the office. Skylar had been so caught up in Cole's pain and her own biting, wretched disappointment with her uncle that she'd forgotten about him. A small gasp escaped her lips.

Ian turned to look at her, and as he registered her clothes and face, a little of the smug coolness fell away. "What in the world are you doing here?" he snapped.

"This is my niece," Skylar's uncle said. "Why shouldn't she be here? And why do they say you know why she altered her appearance?"

Ian licked his lips. "I have no idea."

"It's over," Skylar said. "By now, Dasha is in custody and Malina Dacho is safe. I've been posing as Katerina for more than twenty-four hours. I'm the girl you drugged in her place. I'm the one you sold to Donald and Esther Kester. By now, the American authorities are all over this, and your parlay into trafficking humans is over."

"So what? Luca will see our police don't touch me, and Americans have no power here. Besides, I have an escape plan in motion. In fact, Luca, if you will be so kind as to hand me that envelope, I think we can put our association to an end." He extracted a long envelope from his own breast pocket and offered it as if in exchange.

Skylar's uncle looked down at the envelope he'd laid on his desk.

"What's in it, Uncle?"

It took him forever to answer, and when he did, his voice sounded hollow. "Money."

"In exchange for what?"

"For proof," Cole said. He looked at Banderas and added, "You came across proof that Futura killed the ambassador, didn't you?"

"Oh, I came across far more than that."

"He found Smirnoff's records after he died," Skylar's uncle said, his voice devoid of emotion. "The man kept scrupulous notes. Mr. Banderas has been selling them back to me while using Smirnoff's hidden facility to make papers and passports to fund his own operation."

"It's been very profitable," Banderas said. "Now, hand me the last of the money in exchange for the pages about the death of Lenora Roman."

Skylar's uncle shook his head, but then his gaze focused on a point beyond Skylar's shoulder and his expression crumbled.

Skylar turned to find her aunt standing at the door. This whole thing was unfolding like acts on a stage, each following the other, one person appearing, then another and another.

Aunt Eleanor looked ethereal standing there in a long, flowing robe, almost like a ghost, her skin so pale, her body so thin she might be more thought than substance. Her voice was equally spectral as she whispered, "You've let him blackmail you, Luca?"

"I've had no choice," he said.

She stared at Banderas for a fraction of a second, and then with more strength and more speed than anyone would have thought possible for such a frail woman, raised her arm, withdrawing from the folds of her gown a small gun that she pointed at Banderas. He started to rush her, and she pulled the trigger. The shot boomed in the closed room, and Banderas fell to the floor.

Cole immediately went to check on him. Skylar, aghast, looked from her uncle's shocked expression to her aunt and found the latter had fainted and was lying in a swirl of pale yellow silk. She and her uncle arrived at her aunt's side about the same time, but Skylar stood back as Uncle Luca gathered his wife in his arms.

"All this for covering up a murder of a woman a lifetime ago," Skylar whispered into the profound silence. "If you'd just owned up, none of this would have happened."

By then Cole had joined her, shaking his head as though to relate that Banderas hadn't made it. They both listened as her uncle sang the lullaby he'd been singing his whole life. "No worries, my darling, just sleep." His voice caught, and he swallowed as he looked up at them. "I didn't kill Lenora," he said. "I loved her. I would have married her."

"But you were already married—"

"I met her right after my marriage. She was so young and beautiful. She cleaned my office. I was weak. I had to have her. But I didn't kill her."

"Then who—"

Cole caught her hands. She'd seen the same look in his eyes once before and that's when he'd told her about her uncle. "I think maybe your aunt killed her," he said softly.

"No," Skylar said, shaking her head. "That's not possible."

Tears sparkled in her uncle's eyes. "He's right. When I told Eleanor that Lenora was pregnant, she confronted her and they fought. Eleanor had just found out she couldn't have children…she couldn't handle Lenora having my baby."

"I don't believe this," Skylar said.

"It's the truth," her uncle said. "Eleanor strangled Lenora. She was so strong back then. When she admitted to me what she'd done, I knew I had to protect her. It was my fault, all my fault, and I couldn't let her suffer."

"So you killed an innocent man and his wife?"

"Lenora's father told Charles I had murdered his daughter. Charles would have unearthed the truth. He was a very clever man, and he never took anything at face value. If he'd dug deeper, he would have figured out it was Eleanor. Oh, God, Mary and the kids weren't supposed to be home. And then everything just kept getting worse."

"So you and Smirnoff framed the Roman family for the ambassador's murder and spirited away the children."

"I wanted them all to disappear, and Alexie made it happen. He was brilliant with falsifying records and creating bogus documents. The only one we kept tabs on was the oldest, but he'd lost his memory and didn't seem to present much of a threat. When he came back here years later, it became clear we had to get rid of the family that raised him and, ultimately, him, too. Smirnoff was a very…competent man."

"And then after his death, Banderas found his records and came up with the plan to ship young girls away with fake American passports," Cole said.

"Ian immediately sensed the value of the records when it came to manipulating me," Luca said. "But there's a limit to my wealth and he wanted more." He shook his head. "I should have killed the little bastard when I had the chance."

Skylar turned into Cole's arms and buried her head against his chest. Her aunt had done what her uncle couldn't. She'd pulled the trigger.

Epilogue

Five months later, the Hunt Ranch in Montana

Cole put a hand down, which Skylar caught. He pulled her up into the saddle to sit before him, nuzzling the back of her neck with his nose, breathing in the scent of her. She leaned back against him and sighed.

He'd been on Tyler's ranch for several weeks now, as had John and Paige, who were getting married in the morning. He'd met Tyler's wife, and their newborn son whom they'd named Charles, and Tyler's adoptive mother, Rose. For the first time in his life, he'd been part of what felt like a real family, found a bum knee didn't keep him from enjoying riding and roping and that he seemed to have a natural flair for both.

And Rose had declared that as far as she was concerned, she now had three sons, and this ranch was their home.

All that had been missing was Skylar, who had remained in Kanistan to help her aunt and uncle sell the gallery. The fallout from Banderas's scheme had caused a countrywide scandal and the demand that every child shipped overseas be found and returned. Skylar had helped with that, too, but now she was back in the States and said she wouldn't go back to Kanistan.

"I can't bear to watch them anymore," she said now. "My aunt and uncle, I mean. Their whole lives together have been built on lies. I always thought my aunt was so strong, but she was weak. She knew what Luca did to protect her, and she kept silent."

"And now she's surviving cancer to go to jail," Cole said.

"She won't go to jail. They'll drag this thing out forever. My father is supporting her because she's his sister, but I can't. Neither of them are taking responsibility, and frankly, every time I think of what they did to you and your brothers, I get angry all over again." She took a steadying breath. "I don't want to be a part of it anymore."

"I don't blame you."

"You know I had to let my apartment in L.A. go when I stayed overseas so long?"

"Yes. I'll help you find a new place to live." With him, for instance.

"Well, Rose said you're staying here a few more months and that I was welcome to stay as well. She's offered me room and board in exchange for designing a line of Western wear. We're going to open a little boutique for the guests. Who knows where it will lead? All I know is I'm excited to get back to my own life."

"That's great," he said.

"And Malina is coming for a visit later in the summer, and your brother said we'd all ride into the mountains and go camping. I've spent quite a bit of time with her, and she's really a nice girl. Her grandmother has stepped forward to help her."

Cole gently kicked the horse and began riding toward

the nearby river. "You'll have to teach us all a few words so we can communicate with her."

She turned to look at him. Her hair was its natural color again and longer. He liked the bright orange streak behind her left ear and the way the June breeze blew tendrils around her lovely face. "That would be fun." She sighed heavily and relaxed in his arms. "I can't tell you how wonderful it is to be with you again. It's been a terrible past few months, and I wondered if we'd drift apart—"

"Never," he said. "You're mine."

"I kind of like the sound of that," she said, hugging him, then laying her head back against his shoulder again. They'd only had one night together since she returned, and though it had been as magical as always, he was aching for more. That would never change.

He stopped the horse suddenly, abandoning his big plan to ask her to marry him at John's wedding.

She turned to face him again. "Is something wrong?"

He dug in his pocket and found what he was looking for. His gaze stayed glued to her face as she watched him open his palm.

"Oh, Cole," she said.

"Will you wear it?" he asked, suddenly sure she would accuse him of moving too fast again, of wanting to wait until things were settled.

"Yes, of course I will," she said, holding out her hand. He slipped the ring over her finger where it sparkled like the blue diamond it was. Still, it couldn't compete with her eyes.

"You understand I'm asking you to marry me," he said, wanting things to be clear.

A grin sprang to her succulent lips. "Yes, I know."

"Sooner rather than later, too. I don't want to spend another minute without you."

"Not another minute," she said, throwing her arms around his neck. "There have been far too many minutes without you already. I love you, Cole."

The horse ambled along on its own accord as they lost themselves in each other.

* * * * *

COMING NEXT MONTH from Harlequin® Intrigue®
AVAILABLE FEBRUARY 5, 2013

#1401 ULTIMATE COWBOY
Bucking Bronc Lodge
Rita Herron

A tough cowboy determined to find his missing brother... An FBI agent who blames herself for the boy's disappearance... A ruthless criminal they're determined to catch.

#1402 HOSTAGE MIDWIFE
Cassie Miles

Entrusting her life to playboy Nick Spencer, midwife Kelly Evans has one chance to rescue eight hostages, including a newborn, from an office building rigged with explosives.

#1403 PROTECTING THE PREGNANT PRINCESS
Royal Bodyguards
Lisa Childs

A pregnant princess needs protecting, and royal bodyguard Aaron Timmer is just the man for the job. But in order to protect Charlotte Green, Aaron first has to find her.

#1404 GUARDIAN RANGER
Shadow Agents
Cynthia Eden

Veronica Lane knows that Jasper Adams isn't the type of man she should fall for...but the ex-Ranger is the only man who can keep her safe when she's targeted for death.

#1405 THE MARSHAL'S WITNESS
Lena Diaz

When her identity is leaked to the mob, a woman in Witness Protection must go on the run in the Smoky Mountains with her U.S. Marshal protector.

#1406 DANGEROUS MEMORIES
Angi Morgan

A U.S. Marshal vows to protect a witness with repressed memories while solving her parents' murders, discovering what's truly important in life and rekindling their passion.

You can find more information on upcoming Harlequin® titles, free excerpts and more at www.Harlequin.com.

HICNM0113

REQUEST YOUR FREE BOOKS!
2 FREE NOVELS PLUS 2 FREE GIFTS!

◆HARLEQUIN®

INTRIGUE®

BREATHTAKING ROMANTIC SUSPENSE

YES! Please send me 2 FREE Harlequin Intrigue® novels and my 2 FREE gifts (gifts are worth about $10). After receiving them, if I don't wish to receive any more books, I can return the shipping statement marked "cancel." If I don't cancel, I will receive 6 brand-new novels every month and be billed just $4.49 per book in the U.S. or $5.24 per book in Canada. That's a savings of at least 14% off the cover price! It's quite a bargain! Shipping and handling is just 50¢ per book in the U.S. and 75¢ per book in Canada.* I understand that accepting the 2 free books and gifts places me under no obligation to buy anything. I can always return a shipment and cancel at any time. Even if I never buy another book, the two free books and gifts are mine to keep forever.

182/382 HDN FVQV

Name _____ (PLEASE PRINT) _____

Address _____ Apt. # _____

City _____ State/Prov. _____ Zip/Postal Code _____

Signature (if under 18, a parent or guardian must sign)

Mail to the **Harlequin® Reader Service:**
IN U.S.A.: P.O. Box 1867, Buffalo, NY 14240-1867
IN CANADA: P.O. Box 609, Fort Erie, Ontario L2A 5X3
**Are you a subscriber to Harlequin Intrigue books
and want to receive the larger-print edition?
Call 1-800-873-8635 or visit www.ReaderService.com.**

* Terms and prices subject to change without notice. Prices do not include applicable taxes. Sales tax applicable in N.Y. Canadian residents will be charged applicable taxes. Offer not valid in Quebec. This offer is limited to one order per household. Not valid for current subscribers to Harlequin Intrigue books. All orders subject to credit approval. Credit or debit balances in a customer's account(s) may be offset by any other outstanding balance owed by or to the customer. Please allow 4 to 6 weeks for delivery. Offer available while quantities last.

Your Privacy—The Harlequin® Reader Service is committed to protecting your privacy. Our Privacy Policy is available online at www.ReaderService.com or upon request from the Harlequin Reader Service.

We make a portion of our mailing list available to reputable third parties that offer products we believe may interest you. If you prefer that we not exchange your name with third parties, or if you wish to clarify or modify your communication preferences, please visit us at www.ReaderService.com/consumerchoice or write to us at Harlequin Reader Service Preference Service, P.O. Box 9062, Buffalo, NY 14269. Include your complete name and address.

HI13

SOLDIER UNDER SIEGE

"How *did* you find me, Eva? I'm not exactly listed in any
phone books."

She rested her suddenly shaky hands on her knees. "Someone told me you might be able to help me, so I decided to
track you down. I'm…well, let's just say I'm very skilled when
it comes to computers."

His jaw tensed.

"You're good, too," she added with grudging appreciation.
"You left so many false trails it made me dizzy. But you slipped
up in Costa Rica, and it led me here."

Tate let out a soft whistle. "I'm impressed. Very impressed, actually." He made a tsking sound. "You went to a lot of trouble to find me. Maybe it's time you tell me why."

"I told you—I need your help."

He raised one large hand and rubbed the razor-sharp stubble coating his strong chin.

A tiny thrill shot through her as she watched the oddly seductive gesture and imagined how it would feel to have those calloused fingers stroking her own skin, but that thrill promptly fizzled when she realized her thoughts had drifted off course again. What was it about this man that made her so darn aware of his masculinity?

She shook her head, hoping to clear her foggy brain, and met Tate's expectant expression. "Your help," she repeated.

"Oh really?" he drawled. "My help to do what?"

God, could she do this? How did one even begin to approach something like—

"For Chrissake, sweetheart, spit it out. I don't have all night."

She swallowed. Twice.

He started to push back his chair. "Screw it. I don't have time for—"

"I want you to kill Hector Cruz," she blurted out.

Will Eva's secret be the ultimate unraveling of their fragile trust? Or will an overwhelming desire do them both in? Find out what happens next in SOLDIER UNDER SIEGE

Available February 2013 only from Harlequin Romantic Suspense wherever books are sold.

Rediscover the Harlequin series section starting December 18!